MAYBE HIM

MAYBE HIM

MAYBE THIS TIME

JOLIE MOORE

This edition published by

Moore Digital Media Inc
1125 N Fairfax Avenue
#46071
West Hollywood, CA 90046

Cover Designer: Cover Me Darling
eISBN: 978-1-64414-077-2
ISBN: 978-1-64414-078-9

ALSO BY JOLIE MOORE

Maybe Baby

Maybe Him

Maybe Again

Maybe Now

Maybe You

Taming the Bad Boy

The Secrets She Keeps

Her Secret Crush

What Was Perfect

What Was Lost

What Was True

Release

First Must Burn

Fifty First Dates

for Amie

ONE

SOPHIE REID'S car inched onto the Laurel Canyon entrance ramp, slowing to the usual crawl to enter the Hollywood freeway heading east. The hot, dry Santa Ana winds blew across the San Fernando Valley, causing waves of heat to shimmer on the asphalt. She flipped down her visor and looked at herself in the mirror while waiting for the cars to creep through the traffic light at the top of the ramp. She snapped her fashionably oversized shades over her gray eyes and smiled, knowing she looked good enough to catch everyone's attention. She pushed the appropriate button with her French manicured finger, and the convertible top glided down with a whisper.

On a whim, she had dyed her chin length bob sunflower yellow to match the color of her new Volkswagen Beetle convertible, and she felt like showing off a little. She'd gone braless as usual, and wore a raspberry-colored Henley top adorned with rhinestone buttons. She even gave a pageant style wave to the person behind her who had laughed and pointed at her vanity license plate. EW A BUG. It got her, and the car, a lot of attention, and she liked it that way.

When more than a few minutes had passed and Sophie hadn't moved but a few centimeters, she was sorely tempted to bang ineffectively on her horn to try to get the cars to move faster. At this snail's pace, her good mood was fading fast. She had left her house with little time to spare, forgetting about the ominous back-to-school traffic that jammed the already clogged freeways every September. Now she started to worry that her late arrival would delay the filming of the television show she worked on. The idea of an entire production team of at least hundred people waiting for her arrival made her hands sweat. Sophie shunned a lot of traditional values, but punctuality was not among them.

After what seemed an interminable wait, she finally moved from the entrance ramp onto the actual 101 freeway only to find the traffic at almost a complete stand-still. She looked at the car's cute little dashboard clock and knew she was going to be very, very late to the studio for her call time unless she did the improbable — got across six lanes of stopped traffic and onto the Ventura freeway to speed her way to Burbank. Looking at the clock again, then her watch, as if the large-faced man's timepiece on her wrist would give her a different time, she groaned in frustration.

Berating herself for leaving too late and taking the freeway rather than the street, she fished in the large orange tote bag on the passenger seat for her mobile phone, ready to make her excuses. She noticed that almost everyone was out of his or her car, and the freeway had come to a grinding halt.

"Hey, what's going on?" she called to an older woman who had exited her Bentley and nimbly sprinted past several cars wearing a designer business suit and four-inch Jimmy Choo heels.

"There's a dog on the road," she said breathlessly, only pausing for the briefest of moments to answer. "We're trying to catch him before he gets run over."

It was then that she saw it. A little red fur ball of a dog ran in between the stopped cars, and dodged every single one of the people who tried to catch him—or her. She stopped worrying whether she would be able to complete the actors' make-up in time for the filming. The long-dormant animal lover in Sophie awoke, and propelled her out of the car to join in the canine pursuit. The thought of seeing an innocent dog killed on the road scared the hell out of her. With no regard for her personal safety, she ran after the dog. After five minutes darting around the free-way, she and a tall, impossibly broad-shouldered, sandy-haired man were able to corral the dog between them-selves and their cars. When he moved to grab the dog, it ran toward her, and she triumphantly scooped the warm body into her arms. The dog's heart beat a million miles a minute against hers. She cradled the scared reddish-brown puppy and tried to calm it.

The handsome stranger waved at the frantic Ange-lenos, "She's got him." He paused, looking at her hair, then her car, and smiled. "Hey, Sunflower," he said, nicknaming Sophie for her bright yellow hair. "You want me to take him?"

Sophie buried her nose in the dog's fluffy head, breathing in the warm dog smell. "No I've got him. Can you just hold him while I put my top up?" After handing over the wiggly bundle of fur, she sat back down in her car and raised the convertible's roof to keep the dog secure when she got back on the road. She didn't think her heart, or the dog's, could take a repeat performance. When she turned around to take the dog, a cheer went up from the crowd who were now getting back into their cars, and getting back to the business of driving to work and school.

Their hands touched only briefly when the man handed over the dog, but she felt a jolt that zinged her to the tips of her wild berry toenails. The energy, decidedly sexual, was nothing like she'd ever experienced. It traveled up her arm and zapped her somewhere down low. She grasped the dog-cum-security blanket more securely and looked into the stranger's midnight blue eyes for the first time.

He was looking at her intently, curiously, sizing her up. It was probably the hair, she figured, not her. Men like him did not look twice at women like her. Her multiple piercings and tattoos shocked a lot of conservative types. For just a moment she forgot the furry bundle wiggling in her arms. She felt an unexpected attraction to the man dressed in a starched button down shirt and pressed slacks. His whole demeanor screamed uptight lawyer or bean counting CPA—just the kind of guy she worked to studiously avoid.

The traffic started moving. To be safe, they both

retreated to their cars, but Sophie could not shake the strong and instant connection she felt to the stranger.

He seemed just as bewildered. "Hey, Sunflower, I didn't get your name."

She smiled, trying to hide the shivers he caused. Her usual sarcastic rejoinder froze on her lips. "I'll be fine. Thanks, really, thanks for your help," Sophie said, her gravelly voice more husky than usual, deliberately leaving the question unanswered. She cut the exchange short, knowing that any further conversation with this guy, no matter how handsome his strong features were, no matter how well he filled out the conservatively cut clothes, was a bad, bad idea. She placed the dog on the passenger seat with only an inkling of regret that she hadn't found out his name.

The dog scooted over the gearshift and into the cramped backseat, making itself into as small a ball as possible. In the rearview mirror, she could see the puppy was shaking uncontrollably. She needed to do something quickly. The young stars of her TV show could wait. The dog couldn't.

Unsure of where to go or what to do, Sophie pulled off the next exit at Tujunga Avenue and parked in the shade of a leafy ficus to gather her thoughts. Quickly, she flipped through her mental file, realizing she'd often passed an emergency veterinary clinic on Ventura when driving down the boulevard. Mentally crossing her fingers, she drove south along Tujunga taking a right on Ventura—the clinic was exactly where she remembered, and she parked across the street. Carefully, she pried the quivering puppy from the backseat and held the collarless dog as tightly as she dared crossing the busy street.

NOW HE'D GONE STALKER. Ryan Becker had never followed a woman before without her knowledge. Today did not seem like a good day to start his career as a creepy guy who couldn't take no for an answer, but here he was. He tried to convince himself that this was different. He felt bad for that dog, and didn't think it was right to leave the responsibility to that yellow-haired woman just because she'd been the one to catch the dog.

SOPHIE WAS STANDING at the door of the clinic trying to figure out how she was going to lever open the heavy door and hold on to the dog at the same time when a strong arm pulled the handle for her. She looked back just in time to see the man from the freeway holding the door for her.

"Hello again, Sunflower, I couldn't let you go through this alone," the attractive stranger said, his near perfect smile a little awkward.

Part of her was secretly pleased to see him—if that tingly feeling in her belly was anything to go by. But she was also annoyed because the stranger being here made it much harder to ignore or forget the feelings he'd so quickly aroused in her. The two feelings warred within her for a moment, but she couldn't decide which won the battle, so instead of deciding, she stepped into the clinic's waiting room. He followed her in and, avoiding the crush of people near the reception counter, sat down on the solid wooden benches along the wall.

Sophie turned and looked directly into his dark blue eyes, sizing him up.

"Mmmm…a big, strong guy like you can surely handle him while I check in," she said, handing him the dog before he could protest.

As soon as he gathered the distressed dog on his lap and made a space for himself on the bench, it promptly urinated on his very neatly pressed dress pants. One of the clinic staff people rushed over with paper towels and a spray bottle of disinfectant, and Sophie unsuccessfully hid her laugh behind her hand at the way the man was holding the dog under its front legs like it was a smelly baby, his arms outstretched as far as they would go.

Though she wanted nothing more than to snatch up the wiggling dog and send the nerve-jarring hunk on his way, Sophie held her ground. It was far more interesting to see what he would do next. She predicted he would make up a bogus excuse and be out of the clinic in a heart-beat—Sophie was one hundred percent sure this man did not get urinated on too often.

To her surprise, he handled the incident with aplomb. He blotted his pants with one of the proffered terry cloth towels, then wrapped the small dog gently in another towel and placed it back on his lap. She pulled her gaze from the commotion surrounding the man when the reception-ist's voice caught her attention. At the scrub-garbed woman's request, she took the clipboard and filled in her contact information. When she came to the place where she had to put in a name for the dog, she hesitated a moment and then wrote in "Sasha." It wasn't that she didn't plan to return the dog to its rightful owner, who would, of course, know the dog's real name, it was just that calling a dog "It" was too impersonal.

She sat down next to the man and scratched the dog between the ears, loving the feel of the thick, soft fur under her fingers. It had been years since she'd stroked a dog like this. She hadn't realized how much she'd missed it.

The man pulled his right hand from under the dog and reached out to shake hers. "I don't think we're exactly strangers anymore. I'm Ryan Becker, by the way." Sophie shook his hand, his grip firm and sure, all the while giving him a cool appraising look.

"I'm… " As she was about to respond, the rap song ringtone of her cell phone interrupted. She reluctantly extracted her hand from his. "Hey, Sam," she answered, speaking into the phone. "I'm so sorry…did you get my message? No…can you take care of the kids today? I'm having a bit of an emergency…I'll explain later… Okay, bye," she said flipping the phone closed.

RYAN WAS CRESTFALLEN by the sudden turn of events. This woman, to whom he was strangely attracted, wasn't even available. It sounded like she was married and had kids, for Christ's sake. He looked pointedly at her ring finger. It was devoid of any ornamentation, although many of her other fingers were covered with thick silver bands. Maybe she was the kind of woman who shunned the idea of a wedding band. She certainly didn't appear conventional by any other measure.

Had he severely misjudged what had happened back there on the freeway? What had he been thinking, following her? Her husband would surely take a serious dislike to Ryan's stalker behavior. The lawyer in him knew that he should diffuse the situation before it got out of hand, especially now that she knew his name and could give the police a good description. He strictly adhered to the cliché that the best defense was a good offense.

He absently stroked the puppy while looking at her. "Um, so your husband Sam is home taking care of your kids today?" he asked tentatively.

SOPHIE LAUGHED ALOUD THEN. She couldn't keep it in, even though his handsomely chiseled face looked so disappointed. She hadn't enjoyed this kind of hearty, belly-deep laugh in a long time. Imagining herself with a husband and kids tickled her pink. When she stopped snorting and giggling, she looked at Ryan. "Sam is my very, very gay assistant. I'm the key makeup artist on a kids' cable television show. The 'kids' I was referring to are the older-than-their-years young adult actors who play teenage kids on the show."

Ryan smiled—with relief?—and had just opened his mouth to say something when a man came in with a tiny Jack Russell terrier puppy.

In response to the receptionist, he said, "I don't know how old she is. Some teenagers were selling the dog for drug money at a gas station in the desert—we gave them a hundred bucks just to save the dog."

She scribbled something on a pad of paper. "Name?" she asked, her voice an impatient monotone.

"We're calling her Jane Russell," the man said, smirking.

Sophie couldn't decide whether to laugh or cry. She was relieved that the dog was okay, but the up and down emotions of waiting in the emergency ward were quickly getting to her. She could only hope that no dog came rushing in on a gurney, ER style. She sat quietly next to Ryan while the large flat screen TV quietly played a twenty-four hour news channel.

The receptionist called several humans in succession, referring to them by the name of the pet they brought in. "Rowdy" had overdosed on chocolate, ice cream, and bananas when his owners had left their sundaes on the coffee table. "Bandit" had stolen away from home chasing after a female dog and had torn a gash in his leg trying to climb back under the fence to his yard before his owners returned. "Fluff," a small male tuxedo cat with a decidedly feminine name, refused to eat, and looked painfully thin. Both mirth and misery bubbled just under the surface as other ill and injured pets were admitted to the hospital.

Based upon the hospital's triage, Sophie guessed they'd be waiting for a bit. Sasha had no serious problems that she could see.

"Ryan, you can go now, really. I've already blown a day of work, no need for the both of us to lose out."

The dog, exhausted from his early morning adventure, lay dozing across their legs, which were now touching, the crowded bench having pushed them together. Sophie wanted to attribute the heat she felt stealing up her leg and side to the dog, to the heat of the day, to anything but her attraction to this man.

"I'm here for the long haul," he said with unquestionable finality. "You still haven't told me your name. Another man may think you were avoiding the question."

She was saved from answering when the receptionist called. "Sasha? The doctor is ready to see you now."

The receptionist held open the door for her and Ryan. Sophie picked up the dog and took him to the inner sanctum. The assistant led them to a small examining room, an impersonal metal table bolted to the wall. It looked a lot like a regular doctor's office, except everything was on a much smaller scale. There was a smaller version of the waiting room bench, a smaller flat screen TV, and a few magazines, but still no vet. They squeezed in together on the small bench. With the door closed, however, she was able to free the dog from the confines of the towel, and it sniffed around the sides of the antiseptic room, inspecting the smells only a canine nose could sense.

"You named the dog?" Ryan asked, watching it scamper around the room as it became less anxious and picked up speed.

"I needed to put something down on the form," she said somewhat defensively.

"Hey, I was just wondering how you picked that name," he said, soothing her ruffled feathers.

"There was this big Husky in my neighborhood named Sasha when I was a kid. I used to love to pet him and hang out with him when he escaped from his yard. This dog kind of reminds me of him."

"On the subject of names… " Ryan began, but the door swung open and an older gray-haired woman walked in. She deftly scooped up the dog in one hand and held out the other to shake theirs. "I'm Dr. Emily Blythe."

She placed the dog on the table and held it firmly while examining its eyes, ears, and teeth.

"It says here that you found Sasha on the freeway?"

"He was running through traffic and a bunch of people tried to catch him. I was the lucky one, I guess. Is he going to be okay? How do we find his people?" Sophie rushed on eagerly.

"Well, first," Dr. Blythe said chuckling, "*he* is actually a *she*."

"Oh, okay. Well, how old is she?" Ryan asked.

The veterinarian lifted Sasha's lips and shone a penlight across her pink gums and sharp canine teeth. "She appears to have all forty-two of her permanent teeth. I'd guess that she's about nine or ten months old. In terms of breed, I'd say she looks a lot like a Finnish Spitz." The veterinarian got a device from a shelf that looked like a handheld grocery scanner and ran it along the dog's back and scruff.

"She has no microchip," she said to them. To the dog she said, "You're a little mystery, my dear Sasha."

The doctor continued to examine the dog and Ryan looked at Sophie questioningly.

"So," Sophie asked. "What do we do now?"

"The city law gives you a couple of options," she said matter-of-factly. "You can turn her over to the pound, and if all goes well her owner will find her. Otherwise, she will be available for adoption in four or five days. Or you can keep her and post flyers around the neighborhood where you picked her up, trying to find her owner. It's up to you guys, but I'll hand her off to you with a good bill of health." The veterinarian scribbled some notes in a folder and left the room as briskly as she had entered.

"Do you think we should keep Sasha while we look for the owner?" Ryan asked her.

Sophie paused, thinking about his question. Even though she'd known him for less than an hour, she felt close to him. Quietly she answered, "Honestly, part of me would like to, but I think taking this little cutie to the pound would be the right thing to do. I wouldn't want to get too attached while fostering her."

"But what if no one claims her?"

"Do you want her? Do you have a dog already?" Then she looked at his clothes and shook her head. "Obviously you don't," she said emphatically. "You look like the kind of person who's never had a speck of lint on his clothes, much less blonde dog hair." Sophie scratched between the reddish blond upright ears. "Someone will claim her or adopt her. How could they not?" she said as the dog yawned and tucked herself more securely into Sophie's arms.

"I'll drive you to the pound right now. That way we can drop off the dog and make sure she's safe," Ryan said as if this were some kind of executive crisis to be managed.

So-called alpha males rankled Sophie. She'd grown up with a father who'd issued commands, and she did not like take-charge men to decide what she was going to do next —even when their ideas were good ones. She fumed silently…then pouted. "Why do we have to go together? I'm perfectly capable of driving all by myself." Her words came out with more of a whine than she'd intended. When he didn't budge, she continued. "How do I know you're not some pervert? Maybe this is all a ruse to kidnap me or something. This button-down thing you have going on here," she said gesturing at him, "could all be an act."

"You don't have to worry about that. Sassy makeup artists are not my type." She shot him a look of mock outrage. Ryan smiled in return. His tone oozed reason-ableness. "Look Sunflower, we don't have a leash. She can get squirmy, and I don't want to have to worry about you crashing that brand new car of yours. Let's just see this thing through."

Sophie didn't argue. He didn't come across like a mass murderer. If documentaries were anything to go by, he wasn't charming enough. She had her cell phone. If she admitted it to herself, she wanted to spend more time with him—even though he wasn't her usual type. The fluttery feeling in her stomach was annoying, downright irritating to tell the truth, but in a tiny corner of her brain, she had to admit that it felt good to spend time with a man she was attracted to—even if nothing was ever going to come from it.

"All right, I'm in," she said while opening the passenger door.

In Ryan's low-slung car, they followed the directions the receptionist had given them—back along the freeway, then north on Van Nuys, a boulevard aesthetically caught between its 1950s roots and its current immigrant residents.

They pulled up to the public facility. Sophie was surprised at how modern and clean it looked. The only way it was distinguishable from any other new municipal building was the incessant barking of the dogs in the indoor/outdoor cages. Ryan opened her car door as Sophie held Sasha tight. His chivalry continued as he opened the other doors leading to the shelter's cavernous lobby. It was too bad he wasn't her type. He seemed like a nice guy, and a single girl in Los Angeles could always use more nice guys in her life.

Nothing about the squeaky clean, blue-speckled linoleum floors or sparkling white walls of the shelter suggested it was a home for wayward Los Angeles animals. She'd expected something more akin to a turn of the century orphanage with worn tiles and grimy floors. The large reception area and the adjoining educational center were empty save for one man pushing a dust mop across the already clean floor, and a couple of uniformed officials behind the counter.

Sophie handed the dog to Ryan and looked at the two people dressed like prison guards, a man and a woman. They fit into her vision of an animal shelter much better. The substantially built woman ambled forward. "Can I help you guys?" Her name tag identified her as Hortencia G.

"We're here to drop off a dog," Sophie said.

The woman reached beneath the counter and pulled out a clipboard. "Is he yours or a stray?"

"He's a stray, I guess. I...um, I mean we," Sophie

stammered, inexplicably nervous. "We found him running on the 101 this morning."

Hortencia nodded knowingly. "Yeah, we saw that snarl on KCAL Nine from their helicopter camera. You guys caused quite a tie up on the freeway this morning."

"Yeah, it was something. We certainly never made it into work," Sophie said.

"You're doing the right thing by dropping this dog off. With all the TV coverage this morning, I'm sure his owners will come to claim him." Sophie didn't bother correcting the dog warden about the dog's gender. "Just fill out these forms here," she said, handing Sophie a pen. Sophie wrote down her personal information and what she'd learned about the dog from the vet, while Ryan handed the dog over to the male shelter worker who'd yet to say a word.

Sophie signed her name to the bottom of the form. Horrified, she watched the man put the dog into a contraption similar to a dumbwaiter. As soon as Sasha was in the small metal chute, he closed the stainless steel door with a snap and threw the bolt into place. It was as if Sasha were going to jail. Sophie pushed the forms forward and ran outside without a backward glance toward Ryan. She had a sudden and desperate need for fresh air.

She had pulled her large sunglasses off her head and down onto her nose to cover her eyes when Ryan eventually emerged. Attempting a casual pose, Sophie leaned against the car, legs crossed at the ankles, trying to look for all the world like she was taking in the sun on a warm day.

But Ryan didn't seem fooled. "Hey, you okay?" he asked, his voice only loud enough for her to hear.

Her throat swelled shut as feelings overwhelmed her, and she could not speak. She was not used to feeling this way, and her mind's inability to override her body frustrated her. She just nodded in his general direction.

He grabbed her right hand in his large left one. Its warm strength swallowed hers whole. "Hey, it's not so bad. They said she'll have her own crate back there— food, water, a blanket. It's a hotel for dogs. I'm sure that she'll be home in no time."

"Can we just go?" Sophie choked out, trying unsuccessfully to pull her hand from Ryan's.

He fished the keys from his pocket and popped the locks of the luxury car with a flick of the remote control. He finally let go of her and they got in. The car was quiet save for soft jazz thrumming quietly from about a dozen hidden speakers in the car. Though Ryan took the scenic route, in deference to her need for time to get herself together, she assumed, they were pulling up behind her car on Ventura Boulevard in less than fifteen minutes.

Sophie grasped the door handle to let herself out when Ryan's large male hand on her left arm stilled her movements. Until that moment, she'd been keeping herself together pretty well. She took great pains to hold herself as a confident, assertive woman, and wanted it to remain that way. However, his gentle touch was her undoing. Tears, which she'd held back by sheer force of will, came forth, silently leaking under the oversized dark glasses. She pulled her arm back and pressed her hand, the skin on her knuckles straining with effort, to her mouth, but not in time to stop the sob that escaped.

"I'm sorry," Sophie began, gasping for breath softly. "Leaving Sasha at the pound just made me remember something I've tried to forget."

"What?" he asked, concern obvious in his voice.

When she shook her head, he pulled her hand from her mouth and intertwined their fingers, her small neatly manicured fingers almost disappearing between his larger ones. Distracted by her thoughts, Sophie didn't try to pull away this time. He squeezed her hand reassuringly and he asked again. "What could be so bad that it would make you cry like this over a dog you just met?"

She was quiet for a long time. The hum of the car's air conditioning muffled any sound from outside. When she finally spoke, Sophie's voice was unusually quiet. She looked beyond him as if seeing the past. "I was nine. My mom got me a small white puppy with stick-up ears and lots of fluffy fur, kind of like Sasha." She paused to accept his proffer of a tissue from the surprisingly well-stocked center console, and wiped her nose. "I can't believe I'm telling you this," she said.

Sophie had to admit, though, it was easy talking to him. She chalked it up to him being a total stranger who she would never have to see again, like the person next to you on a plane during bad turbulence. She continued talking, suddenly feeling cathartic.

"Growing up, I'd wanted a dog for years. I just knew it would be my best friend. Not like my older sister Selie who never gave me the time of day. We could play together, sleep together, and go for walks together. I know that all sounds a little weird, but I was kind of a lonely kid.

"Anyway, my parents surprised me with a dog for my birthday. Daisy, that was her name, was a better friend than I expected, but I wasn't that good at training her—so she sometimes went in the house or chewed things she wasn't supposed to. One day, I came home from school to find Dad and Daisy sitting on the front step. My dad didn't look happy. He told me that my mother and he had talked and that the dog wasn't well trained enough to stay with us and that they were bringing her to the pound for a more suitable family to adopt."

"DID HE REALLY TAKE HER BACK?" Ryan asked, amazed that some parents could be so cold. No matter how out of hand he and his brother Cameron had acted—and as two boys with a single mom, it had sometimes gotten really out of hand—he couldn't fathom his mother doing anything that heartless.

She nodded, and a single tear dripped from her small upturned nose. "I ran to my room crying when I heard my father's station wagon drive off. I never saw Daisy again. When that woman put Sasha in that chute today, I could just imagine how lost Daisy must have felt being separated from me and not ever knowing why."

Ryan's heart went out to her. All at once, he realized that the bravado, the crazy hair, and even the outsized earrings were probably nothing more than a hard outer shell to protect the softhearted woman underneath. He put aside his attraction to her for the moment. Ryan wanted nothing more than to soothe the past hurts she must have suffered.

He leaned over the car's center console, pulled the sunglasses gently from her face, and wiped the tears from her soft gray eyes with his thumb forgoing another tissue. Before he could properly weigh his options, or consider her response, he closed the distance between them and kissed her—gently at first on her tear-stained cheek, then brushed her lips with his. Ryan told himself he did it because it was the best way he could think of to make her feel better. However, his soothing intentions quickly escalated into something else. Her lips were softer than he'd imagined. His hand slipped from her face to her breast, so temptingly on offer, covered only by the thin fabric of her shirt.

SOPHIE DIDN'T RESPOND to his kiss at first. It took a few seconds to realize that Ryan was kissing her. Any thoughts of dogs or lingering feelings of sadness fled, and she realized that his lips felt even better than they looked. When his tongue ran against the seam of her lips, she opened for him almost without thinking. He tasted like mint and wanting. She stopped being hesitant, and responded with ardor. It felt good to be kissed like this. She moved to clutch his shirtfront for support, but instead smoothed her hand against it, entranced with the hard chest underneath the once crisp shirt. When his hand stroked her breast, her breath caught in her chest, releasing in a slow hiss.

Reluctantly, it seemed, Ryan pulled away. For a

moment, neither of them said anything. Sophie felt awkward, overwhelmed by the response he'd evoked in her. Her encounters with the opposite sex were usually far less emotional. Looking at his now rumpled shirt and his stained pants covered with dog hair, lint, urine, and God knows what else, she couldn't help herself and laughed. Once she started, she couldn't stop her giggling.

Ryan sat back in his seat, a chuckle or two escaping his sensual but masculine lips.

"This has been nothing if not a crazy morning," she said, trying to quell her laughter.

"Do you want to get coffee, something to eat? I missed my breakfast meeting in Burbank and I'm starving."

Sophie's guard came back up, cloaking her like armor. Both the tears and laughter cleared from her face and the cool mask of indifference she usually wore came over her countenance. "You should eat. I should go," she said. She pulled the door handle and stepped out into the bright sunshine. The hot Valley sun did little to cool her over-heated body.

Ryan pushed open his door quickly and looked at her over the top of the car. "I know we don't exactly know each other. I don't even know your name, Sunflower, but something clicked between us this morning. I think we should—"

"I'm sorry, but you're not my type." The words rushed from her lips. Sophie unlocked her car door. She'd made the mistake of letting her guard down, and everything had gone too far. She needed to get out of there quickly before she did anything else completely out of character. And she really was sorry. But she had a rule against dating tight-

assed suits, no matter how well they filled out that proverbial suit, and she wasn't going to break her number one
tenet. The two of them were a train wreck waiting to
happen. She was a smart girl, and smart girls avoided
train wrecks. "I have to go," she threw over her shoulder
as she slid into her car. She started the Beetle and made a
quick U-turn on Ventura before she could fall into the
depths of his blue eyes and change her mind.

TWO

TWO DAYS LATER, Ryan Becker got up from his high-backed, leather office chair and stretched. His hand-tailored shirt strained against his biceps and outlined his deeply muscled back. He looked out his window toward the mountains that surrounded Malibu. It was an unusually clear day in Los Angeles—neither fog nor smog marred the endless blue skies. He had a fine view of the pleasure piers, the water, and the topography surrounding the area. But neither his long morning meeting in Burbank nor the view could distract him from thinking about the woman with the bright yellow hair. He was one hundred percent sure she'd had the same jolt of awareness he did.

Driving back from Burbank to Venice, across the Ventura and Hollywood freeways, then down the San Diego freeway, he couldn't help looking for her car today as he had every moment on the road for the past two mornings and evenings. Every Volkswagen Beetle caught his distracted eye, the yellow ones made his heart beat a rapid tattoo, and the convertibles made him break out in a sweat. He scrutinized every personalized license plate looking for her unique brand of humor. In a city of almost four million, and a metropolitan area of about ten million, he knew the chances of seeing her ever again were about one in, well, ten million. Still, looking out on the blue horizon, he couldn't help hoping.

SOPHIE'S small house had always seemed like a cozy and welcoming artists' retreat. Suddenly it felt as empty as a funeral parlor, too big and eerily quiet. The house was modest by Los Angeles McMansion standards, but the post-World War II tract house was her pride and joy. Just the simple fact that she'd bought it with her own money gave her a heady sense of accomplishment that no put down from her family could take away.

She had put in a lot of the sweat equity to fix up the house herself, from painting the outside a pleasing butter yellow, to sanding decades' worth of grime and varnish from the narrow oak plank floors. When she was bored or restless, working on some aspect of the house usually took her mind off whatever was bothering her.

But no matter how hard she tried, over the last couple of days, she couldn't shake Sasha from her mind—nor, if she were being honest with herself, could she get images of Ryan's handsome face and gentle nature out of her head. She tried watching TV, but even her usual critique of others' makeup work bored her after a few minutes.

Sophie passed the slightly warped bathroom mirror on her way to the small second bedroom she used as a den. She peered at her distorted reflection in the funky flea market mirror and imagined herself with a nose ring. She had never given that or a tongue piercing much thought, but maybe it was time to reconsider. Instead of going the body mutilation route, she opened a new pack of hair dye and turned her yellow hair purple.

Well, that was one hour down, she thought. She sat down in her hippie era white leather office chair and powered up her MacBook. Scrolling and clicking through headlines on several news websites could not hold her concentration either. Against her better judgment, she found herself Googling the City of Los Angeles Animal Services. When the site came up, she clicked on the East Valley shelter and looked at the dogs that were coming up for adoption. On the third page, there was a picture of Sasha, looking wide-eyed and silly, along with her particulars and the day she would be up for adoption—which, Sophie realized glancing at the calendar on her desk, was tomorrow. The city made found dogs available after only four days. She hoped it had been enough time to find Sasha's true owner.

Sophie found herself in her backyard kicking at the ground stakes, assessing the strength of her fence. She was seriously considering adopting the dog. She didn't know if taking another living being into her home was selfish or impulsive, but she picked up the cordless phone and placed a call to her older sister Selena to hash out her thoughts. Selie was not as great a sounding board as her best friend Holly Prentice, but she knew Sophie's history with animals better than anyone.

"Hey, sis," Sophie said. Her sister Selie was the older, beautiful, and now happily married one in the family.

Their parents loved to gloat about her. She'd done all the right things—finished college at Berkeley, gotten an MBA at UCLA's Anderson school, gone into marketing at Warner Bros. studio, and had a perfectly timed baby. She had achieved the nearly impossible; she had it all. Now she was the vice president of marketing, the perfect mom, and the perfect wife. She lived in a beautiful house just around the corner from their parents. Sophie was sure she heard the clink of her sister's ever-present pearls against the plastic of the receiver. In her mind's eye, Selie was perfectly outfitted in Lilly Pulitzer.

"I'm so glad you called," Selie said.

That was a new one, Sophie thought. She and Selena only talked sporadically even though they lived less than twenty miles apart. "What's up?"

"Well, I'll get to that later," she said, evasively. "What's up with you?"

"I'm thinking about getting a dog."

"Mmmm," Selie said, non-committal.

Sophie told her sister the whole story about finding the dog on the freeway, carefully excising Ryan from the tale.

Selie, always the voice of reason, weighed in without hesitation. "Do you think you can handle a dog with your schedule? What will he do when you're on set for those twelve-hour days?"

"I figure I can hire a dog walker or sitter or ask a neighbor or something. There are a lot of days when I'm off, especially during the spring hiatus or in the winter when productions are slowing down."

"I don't know, Sophie. You should think hard on that one," Selie said, her tone going from friendly to preachy.

"Being a new mother now, I'm realizing how much responsibility another life is." Sophie was glad videophones had never taken off and her sister couldn't see the eye rolling or the gagging motions she was making with her hands and mouth. She would always be the little sister and look up to Selie, but she found her to be a little too self-righteous and patronizing at times. Unfortunately, this was one of those times. She would have to work out her uncertain feelings about Ryan on her own. Her sister would probably push them down the aisle once she found out a 'suit' was interested in her.

Rather than start those same sibling arguments all over again, Sophie decided to let her behavior pass. See, she had maturity. "Thanks," she said a little too unconvincingly. "I'll take your advice into consideration, sis. What's the other thing you wanted to talk about?"

Selie paused for a long time. "Well…Daddy is scheduled to receive a lifetime achievement award from the bar association and I think we should have a reception with all of his friends and colleagues at the house."

"We?" Sophie laughed, unable to hide her incredulity. Her parents never missed a chance to express their disappointment at her life and career choices. "I don't think they envision me being co-host of a party for another of Daddy's endless honors. Besides, my Norma Kamali is at the cleaners."

Selie sighed, the old hurts resurfacing. "It was just a thought, Sophie. I think you and the 'rents need to bury whatever hatchet you guys have between you — or however that metaphor goes."

"I know," Sophie said, closing her eyes and trying to

draw on some reserve of inner calm. "You're right. We're all getting a little too old for this. I'm never going to finish college, and they're never going to have the perfect younger daughter they wanted. The sooner we all settle on that, the better." She paused to clear her thoughts. "Let me think about it. Maybe I can play the perfect daughter for one night. So," she said, abruptly changing the subject back to her original reason for calling. "Do you think I should get Sasha?"

"Who?" her sister asked. Sophie sighed. Why was it so hard for anyone in her family to focus on *her* problems for more than a minute? It was all too easy for them to dismiss anything that concerned her as frivolous.

"The dog, Selie. That's our nickname for her."

"Our? Yours and whose?" Selie said, fully attentive now that her curiosity was piqued. Sophie wanted to kick herself in the ass for that unintentional slip.

"No one, really. There was just a guy who helped me out when I caught her on the freeway," Sophie said doing her best to minimize Ryan's role and avoid any awkward questions.

"Is this guy single?" Selie asked, very much back into the conversation.

"Yes, I think he's single, but he's a suit. And you know I don't do suits."

"Mmmm." Selie packed a lot into her mmmms. "That's too bad. A nice normal boyfriend could do you some good. Anyway, I can't make that doggy decision for you," her sister said, displaying the wisdom of age, or at least the wisdom of being a few years older than Sophie. "But I do know that you can put 'first rights' on the dog, so you can be the first to adopt her if you decide to."

"What are first rights?"

Selie explained the procedure that guaranteed the dog would go to the person who brought her in. Almost decided, Sophie ended that call and placed another call to the animal shelter. With a little trepidation, she forked over her credit card information and paid ten dollars for the right to be able to adopt Sasha when she became available first thing Monday morning.

RYAN HAD COMPLETED his pro and con lists, neatly printed on a thick yellow legal pad, Saturday night. The reasons for bringing Sasha home outnumbered the reasons against. He was getting the dog, and that was that. He had called the shelter and knew Sasha would be available for adoption first thing Monday morning. Ryan would be there bright and early to make sure he was first.

"I'm getting a dog," Ryan announced to his mother and brother at Sunday brunch.

He was the last to arrive to the busy upscale eatery on Ventura Boulevard, Sherman Oaks's restaurant row. His brother had a large mug of steaming coffee, likely his second, and his mother, tap water, per usual. He ordered decaffeinated tea.

"That's cool," Cameron said, clapping him on the shoulder. His mother didn't look as thrilled. "I think you need a wife, not a dog. Someone to take care of you, not something to take care of."

"Mom, it's not like I'm not trying," Ryan said, casting a

sidelong glance at his brother. Cameron shrugged almost imperceptibly, looking happy not to be the brother under scrutiny for once. Cameron was two years older than Ryan and already had one divorce under his belt. His mother had given his brother a reprieve for a little while. Instead she nagged Ryan every chance she got about finding a suitable mate.

The waitress came. He and Cameron ordered eggs — his with turkey bacon and micro greens, his brother's with sausage, bacon, potatoes, and toast. His mother ordered whole-wheat toast, dry. When their waitress took their orders to the kitchen, he shook his head.

"Mom, aren't you hungry? You could have had eggs or pancakes or French toast."

"Ryan, the toast is just fine with me. The food here is too rich for my blood."

"Cam and I always pay when we all go out. You know that."

"It doesn't make me any more comfortable wasting money like this. I could make the two of you eggs for less than a couple of dollars. I'd even throw in the coffee for free," she said. She patted him on the arm. "At least you can afford it," she said, barely concealing a smile. Ryan knew his mother was proud of his and his brother's accomplishments — Cameron had joined the LAPD after high school and had recently made lieutenant two in the vice unit.

But their mother was loathe to give up the frugal way she'd learned to live as a single mother to two boys who could have eaten her out of house and home without her careful budgeting and planning. The unexpected loss of their father's pension and death benefits had made her even more frugal.

Ryan had a huge soft spot for his mom and wanted to please her. She'd sacrificed so much for them, he thought it was their duty to give her what she wanted. That was the only reason he could think of later—when he was kicking himself—for what he said next. "I met someone."

His mother stopped fiddling with the straw in her ice water, her faded blue eyes, sharp with intelligence, focused keenly on him.

"Where did you meet her?"

He told them the tale of rescuing the dog on the freeway and explained that was the dog he was adopting first thing the next morning. And then he mentioned Sunflower, how she bravely rescued the dog with no thought about her personal safety, how she skipped work to take the dog to the veterinarian. Her confession of her childhood pain and the kiss they shared, he kept to himself. It was something he liked to savor in the darkness of the night, in his bed, alone.

Cameron looked up from his eggs for a moment. "What does she do?"

"She's a makeup artist for television," he said.

"Cool," his suddenly monosyllabic brother responded.

His mom, distracted from her normal grumbling, ate her toast and even helped herself to butter and some of his eggs without comment on the cost. "So what's her name? What does she look like? When are you going to bring her by?"

Cameron smirked. "It's never too soon to give her that

grandchild she's always talking about. Yesenia and I certainly failed her there."

Ryan ducked his head, embarrassed. "Um, well, about that... "

"Answer your brother's question. I don't want to die with no grandkids."

"I kind of don't know her name... "

His brother put down his fork and peppered questions like the cop he was. "Her address?" Ryan shook his head. "Her number?" Ryan shook again. "So what exactly do you have?"

He shrugged. "Her license plate."

His mother got up from the table. "Humph. You got me all excited over nothing. I'm going to the ladies' room," she said, stomping off.

After he stopped guffawing, Cameron let loose. "No name, no number. What's the story, man?"

"She said something about me not being her type."

"Mm, and you can't take no for an answer."

"She didn't kiss me like I wasn't *her type*." So much for keeping that a secret. Ryan cleared his throat and lowered his voice. "Do you think you can help me out here?"

Cameron shook his head. "Sorry, dude, I use my special police powers for good, not evil." He waved his fingers in the air like a phony psychic. "You're on your own here. Wish you luck, though," he added, another chuckle escaping.

"Gee thanks," Ryan said facetiously. "I'll find her. Don't worry." There was more conviction in that statement than he felt.

After he dropped his mother off at home, he drove

around town laying in supplies and preparing his house for its newest occupant. At a Studio City pet superstore he picked up a crate, a leash, and a collar. He went to a natural food store in Beverly Hills and bought organic kibble and several varieties of canned dog food that claimed to be just like homemade. Who made the home-made dog food that it was trying to emulate, he wondered.

He stopped by Goodwill and purchased a blanket to protect the leather seats of his Acura. Next, he talked to his neighbors and perused the Internet, searching for available dog walkers in his area. He had interviewed three and hired one. He was, by two o'clock on Sunday afternoon, exhausted, but ready for Sasha.

It was damned hot on Monday morning, and Ryan was sure he was seeing things as waves of heat shimmered from the pavement. The yellow Beetle convertible with the personalized license plate appeared like an apparition before him. Was Sunflower here to adopt Sasha too? He raced into the shelter, and the bright purple hair in the small crowd called to him like a beacon. It wasn't yellow, but the nearly neon color had to be her. He pushed his way to the front of the line and froze, unusually indeci-sive. What was he going to say to her? She solved his dilemma when she turned around unexpectedly to look for something in the small messenger bag looped around her body and resting on her very scrumptious-looking derriere.

"Oh, Ryan, hey there," she said, looking taken aback, her raspy voice sounding a little breathless. "What are you doing here? Are you getting a dog too?"

"I came to get Sasha. I couldn't leave her here after all

your talk of doggie jail. And over the weekend I worked out how I could fit a dog into my life."

"Ma'am," the woman behind the counter called out. "Your dog is ready to pick up." Sunflower turned back to the counter and took the nylon leash he offered, and followed the woman back to the outdoor caged area. A few minutes later, she emerged with Sasha in her arms.

The woman took the paperwork off the counter, dropped it into a disorganized mesh basket, and looked Ryan in the eye. "How can I help you, sir?"

Flustered and holding an empty collar and leash in hand, he said, "I was here, actually, to adopt that same dog."

The woman nodded. "I think I remember you two from the other day. Found the dog on the freeway, right?" When he nodded, she continued. "Well, she got first rights on that dog, so she's eligible to adopt her first. If you're interested, though, we have a whole passel of other dogs that are currently available for adoption and in need of a home." *Maybe*, Ryan thought, but quickly shook his head. He needed to stay with Sunflower and figure out how he could arrange to see her, and that dog, again.

RYAN SPRINTED across the lobby and caught up with Sophie. "Do I at least get visitation rights?"

He looked so eager, she couldn't suppress a laugh. "I don't think Sasha would appreciate the back and forth between two different households. We'd have to work out a schedule, who got weekends, who got holidays…it

would be hard on her. She'd need psychological coun-
seling within the year."

"Do you want to have breakfast or something?" Ryan
asked. "Maybe we can talk about this."

Sophie looked down at Sasha, who calmly lay on the
floor, panting and looking between them as if she didn't
have a care in the world. "Ryan, please don't take this the
wrong way, but I don't think this…is a good idea. It was
nice meeting you, but it was just one of those things. We
should leave it at that. Plus, I'm not hungry."

Sophie was proud of herself for fighting her attraction
to him and tying it all up neatly when her stomach
betrayed her and growled loudly. Damn.

Ryan raised an eyebrow.

"Okay," Sophie agreed. "Maybe a little breakfast."

They agreed to drive separately to a Belgian café that
Ryan recommended. The dog was far calmer than the last
time she was in the car, and hung her head out the
window as Sophie drove. When she passed Moorpark, the
urge to turn and go home was strong. She could stand him
up and never have to deal with the feelings he aroused.
She didn't know what kept her driving south, but she
made the left on Ventura and headed for the breakfast
place. It wasn't like breakfast was a precursor of sex or
marriage. They would have a friendly meal, and no matter
how attractive he was and how much she wanted to kiss
him again, she would go on her merry way.

THE HOSTESS SEATED THEM OUTSIDE, shaded from
the bright September sun by a large umbrella. Sasha

curled up around the umbrella's stand and lapped up the water the waitress brought her. As Sunflower stared at the menu, Ryan looked at her. There was something about this woman that pulled him to her, even though he couldn't put his finger on just what that was.

His normal "type" was a quiet, modest woman who dressed conservatively and spoke softly. He met them at Junior League fundraisers and alumni events. Sunflower, with her nontraditional job, wild hair, and multiple piercings would scare those women into hiding. He wanted to get married, have kids, do all those traditional things. He needed a wife who would stay at home, raise their children. Act as a perfect hostess and companion as he moved up the career ladder. Despite his active pursuit of this mythical partner, he hadn't met that right woman yet.

Intellectually, he knew Sunflower wasn't that person. But he'd willingly take a breather from his pursuit to see where his attraction to her led, and work her out of his system so he could move on with his end game. He'd planned it all out years ago on a series of yellow legal pads, and while he may be momentarily distracted, he wouldn't be deterred from his goals.

The waitress introduced herself and scribbled their order on a small pad. When she'd gone, Sunflower leaned down to check on the dog. Damn, the view was good. It was days like this he loved California. Sunflower was definitely dressed for the hot, late summer weather. She was wearing one of those skimpy exercise outfits that were far too expensive to actually sweat in. The purple top she wore did little to cover her small, pert breasts, not that he was looking. Okay, maybe he had glanced once or twice.

But she wasn't wearing any sort of bra under the scanty tank and all sorts of ideas played in his head.

The top was a strappy thing that left most of her back exposed and he admired her pale skin through the intricate weave. She looked very soft and touchable. It was the first time he realized she had a smattering of freckles across the bridge of her nose. She must have covered them with makeup that other day, though she didn't need a lick of makeup to look good. She also had the sexiest tattoo on her back near her left shoulder. He wondered what the Chinese characters symbolized. He tried not to imagine himself gently kissing those freckles or stroking that tattoo.

When she was done tending to the dog, she sat bolt upright in her chair, probably sensing his gaze.

"What are you looking at?" she asked. She'd caught him staring.

Telling her that he was admiring her skin or imagining himself stroking her cleavage was out. He stammered the first thing that came to his mind.

"I was wondering what that tattoo says." He hoped his face wasn't beet red with embarrassment at his fib.

She stroked her left shoulder reflexively, touching the two calligraphic Chinese characters. "Oh, this. They translate into 'wisdom.'"

"Why wisdom?" he asked tentatively.

"What, you don't see me as a wise woman? Not enough wrinkles yet, huh?" She laughed, smoothing her fingers against her unlined face. "It's the meaning of my name."

"So, when are we going to stop playing these games?

You should just tell me your name now, so we can get that part over with."

FORTUNATELY FOR SOPHIE, the waitress's arrival with their food saved her from having to answer. She'd gotten a chocolate croissant and a large iced latte. He'd ordered an egg white Florentine omelet and bread that seemed to have enough grains and seeds on it to keep up his daily fiber count with one bite. She stirred three sugar packets into her coffee and took a long sip while coolly appraising him.

"On a diet?" she asked. He looked like he worked out —a lot. The collared blue polo shirt stretched across his broad shoulders and flared out where his waist narrowed. She didn't even want to think what the baggy cargo shorts hid below the waist. No doubt it was just as spectacular.

"I like to eat healthy," he answered, taking a huge bite of toast.

She cleared her throat. "Are you a lawyer or an accountant?"

He answered seemingly without thinking. "I'm a lawyer."

Sophie nodded knowingly. "Please don't take what I'm going to say next personally," she said, covering his hand with hers on the small enameled café table. She immediately wished she hadn't touched him. Being near Ryan was like playing with fire, and she'd just gotten singed.

She liked looking at the weekend's worth of stubble on his square jaw, hearing his well-modulated voice, touching his hair roughened skin, and kissing those perfect lips.

Definitely kissing him. *Crap*, she thought, and pulled her hand away. She needed to stop this relationship—or seduction or whatever it was—before she got in too deep. Being with him would be like wading into a calm ocean with a deathly riptide. She'd be in too far before she realized she'd compromised her life. She needed to keep something back. She needed to keep everything back. If she told him her name, it would be the crack in the door. And Sophie knew, he'd come right in.

"You're a nice person from what I see," she continued. "Somewhere out there is a Seven Sisters graduate in pearls who is made for you. I know I'm not your type. We'd be like oil and water, and I don't date lawyers —ever."

She punctuated her comment by taking a big mouthful of pastry. The bite was way too big, she realized far too late. Her smooth brush off was ruined when chocolate went everywhere, and she did her best to catch what she could with her fingers. She was unprepared when Ryan reached across the table and scraped an errant dribble from her lower lip. She shivered as she felt his touch everywhere from her beaded nipples to her tightening womb. She wanted to damn her principles to the wind and give in to the feeling he aroused in her, but she knew better.

He sat back in his chair and smiled at her. The small smile didn't quite reach his sad eyes.

"Sunflower… " He didn't need to say any more. Their attraction to each other was obvious—to them, and probably to anyone within ten feet of them.

"I know. That's why I have to go. I have to get food, a

bed, a collar, a real leash, and whatever else I'll need for Sasha."

"You should come back to my place."

"What?" She must not have heard right. Was that a come on after her brush off?

"There's no need for you to buy all that stuff." He sighed, resigned. "I bought everything yesterday—food, a crate, a strong leather leash, and chew toys."

"Are you going to get another dog?"

"I wanted Sasha," he said. "I wanted you." She could have sworn she heard him utter the last statement under his breath.

"Are you sure?" The real question was implicit in her tone. She wanted to be certain they were on the same page. She would go back to his place for supplies, nothing more.

"Yeah. What the heck."

She should have guessed he lived off one of the more conservative canyon roads. The Hollywood hills divided the city of Los Angeles. They separated the Los Angeles "Basin" from the San Fernando "Valley." Crisscrossing the hills, and connecting the more urban basin to the more suburban Valley, were a number of secluded hillside neighborhoods.

Each pass had a different reputation. Laurel Canyon was a haven for artists and sixties hippies who still clung to the ideals of that generation and decrepit VW buses, while Benedict Canyon was filled with nouveau riche movie and television producers. Coldwater Canyon, on the other hand, housed the bankers, lawyers, and every other suit in Los Angeles. So it was no shock to Sophie that Ryan lived in this area.

At his urging, she brought Sasha into the house. The dog immediately ran over to the full water bowl set out for her, lapping up the liquid happily but noisily, then she plopped down unceremoniously on the dog bed Ryan had carefully placed in a corner of a dining room that was so neat it resembled a movie set.

"Would you like to see the house?" Ryan asked. The dog crossed her front paws primly, and rested her head upon them. Sasha was settled in for the long haul. It sounded like Ryan wanted to show his house off, and the dog wasn't complaining, so Sophie obliged, albeit a little hesitantly.

"Um, sure," she said. The kitchen was a small but ultra-modern affair with a fully stocked wine refrigerator and gleaming new stainless steel appliances. The rest of the house followed suit. Everything was new and clean and somehow not entirely lived in.

"And you were going to bring a dog into this house?" Sophie asked, incredulous. "How were you going to deal with the hair and the inevitable doggy mess she would have left you with?"

"I bought a dust buster," Ryan said, brandishing the new-looking small silver and gray vacuum.

Sophie did nothing to hide her smirk as she looked at him under her purple bangs. The rest of the house was bachelor central. She would never understand, in a million years, why all single men had black leather couches. Ryan's was a black leather sectional, a nod, she guessed, to the recent trend in L-shaped couches. The house was modern with distinct lines, open skylights, and integrated upgrades everywhere. The master bath even had a bidet. A *bidet*, for goodness sakes. She didn't even want to think about that.

The last room he showed her was the master bedroom. She had no idea why the view of a king-sized sleigh bed covered in a flawless tan and navy striped duvet made her warm all over, but she needed to get out of there—fast. She'd get what she came for and go home. Now. She was about to scurry her way out the door and into her car when she barreled into Ryan, who'd been leaning casually against the doorjamb.

He caught her in his strong arms and set her back just a few inches.

"I think I need to get going before I rip your clothes off and take you right here," Sophie said, trying her best to scare him off.

Ryan had the good grace to blush. But her words had the opposite effect. "I think that's an excellent idea," he said, his voice husky. While she was trying to figure out what was a good idea, he kissed her. Sophie's last coherent thought was that in the future she would learn to keep her big mouth shut.

Oh, lordy have mercy on her soul. His mouth felt as good as she remembered. Better. He tasted like the honey in his breakfast tea and warm, masculine heat. Sophie wanted nothing more than to give herself over to the sensation of his sensual lips rubbing hers, having a time honored duel with his tongue. Maybe even do the horizontal mambo. Part of her hoped that with this man, at this time, things would be different. But they wouldn't be. They never were.

Every time a man so much as made a pass at her, touched her, kissed her like Ryan was kissing her, she reacted like an adolescent.

But Ryan's hands had a calming effect. They slid from where they had been caressing her shoulder and moved beneath the tiny straps of her tank. Her nipples puckered in response and Sophie's fear subsided a little, her body softening, yielding to his touch. Ryan moved from kissing her lips to gently brushing her eyelids, her nose, and her forehead with his mouth. She relaxed. They'd covered this ground before. Kissing she could handle.

The panicky feeling subsided until he spoke, and pulled the strap of her tank top aside.

"Oh God, I've been waiting to do this all morning, to taste every last one of those freckles, to have you beneath me," he whispered fiercely.

Sophie was breathing rapidly now, in full panic and retreat mode. Ryan mistook her shortness of breath for passion, and started to propel them toward the bed.

"I have to go, Ryan," Sophie said, pushing hard against his chest. Cool air brushed against her bare skin, and she looked down, noticing for the first time that her top was askew. Embarrassed to see even part of her breast exposed to his intense blue eyes, she stopped on the bedroom threshold and adjusted her tank. "Sasha and I should get home now."

He sighed deeply, audibly. He held his hand against his chest, calming his breath, trying to ease his obvious arousal. She averted her eyes from his tented cargo shorts until his breathing slowed.

"It's not going to happen for us, is it?" he asked, shoving his fingers through his tawny hair, leaving the wavy strands sexily mussed. Her fingers itched and her body throbbed, all clamoring to pull him to her and soothe the ache they both felt. With practiced ease, she pushed the feelings away and turned her back on him, navigating the way to the front door.

"Ryan, it's nothing personal, really," she threw over her shoulder. "Can you help me load the kibble into my car?"

They silently packed the dog stuff into her pint-sized trunk and were barely able to close the lid. She put Sasha in the new collar and attached the multi-colored woven leather leash.

"You're all set, Sunflower."

"Thanks for all your help. You're a truly nice guy, Ryan. I hope you find what you want out there."

"And that can't be us? You can't bend your no-lawyer rule just this one time?"

"I can't," she responded quietly as she buckled herself, then the dog in safely. He'd even thought to buy the dog a harness for car travel. She turned on the car and put it in drive. With her foot on the brake, she spoke with a sense of finality that she hoped she conveyed to Ryan.

"I don't date lawyers, Ryan. And I don't like sex." And with that, she sped off down the windy road.

THREE

WHAT NORMAL PERSON DISLIKED SEX? She sure seemed to appreciate what had been heating up between them in the bedroom. When Ryan finally fought past the cloud of his own arousal, which had blinded him to a lot, he realized that she was somewhat nervous or tense when they were necking like teenagers. He had chalked it up to the fact that everyone was apprehensive their first time with someone new.

Standing in the living area holding his very erect dick was not going to help him figure out what to do, if there was anything to do. He took himself to the shower to do something to ease the ache Sunflower had caused.

SOPHIE WANTED to pull over somewhere on Mulholland Drive and bang her head against the layers of sedimentary rock exposed on the side of the road, but the sheer drops on either side of her car stopped her cold. She'd spent her teen years and her twenties working very hard to cultivate a certain persona. She wanted to be a very sexually confident woman who spoke her mind and could handle her man.

What was wrong with her? Two kisses and one caress from a man and she was putty in his hands, admitting her deepest, darkest secrets to him. Thank goodness he didn't know her name. She'd never have to face him again and relive the humiliating episode in his bedroom. Any other normal woman, she knew, would have just slept with him right then and there. But not her. No siree.

A mere kiss and she froze up like an iceberg. No one used the word frigid anymore. It seemed like a word from a bad 1970s romance novel, but if the shoe fit... She shrugged wearily. The few times she'd been with a guy, it had taken a lot of Dutch courage to get her in the sack. Since she was not exactly sober during the encounters, she didn't remember much, and what she could recall was downright cringe worthy. She was all bark and no bite.

Even if she could get over her sex problem, her anti-lawyer rule was an absolute. She'd lived under her father's thumb for too many years to even go there with a man, no matter how much he wet her whistle. There were hundreds of professions out there, and she'd date anyone from any job—garbage man to CEO—but not anyone who'd passed the bar. She'd had a lifetime worth of uptight, rigid, and controlling men. No matter how nice Ryan seemed on the outside, she'd be a fool to get involved with someone whose profession defined his personal life. She was sure Ryan's pro/con list for the dog and the neater than neat house exemplified exactly what she didn't need in a man.

. . .

TWO WEEKS LATER, Ryan tucked his hand-tailored, button-down, monogrammed shirt into his tan wool pants and debated on whether he should add a sport coat to his ensemble. When he tried on the navy blazer, even he had to admit it made him look ten years older. When did he get so conservative? He felt geriatric compared to Sunflower. Part of him—well, if he were honest with himself, all of him—wished he were spending the evening with her. Thinking about how he would dress for a date with her made him decide to vote a definite "no" on the sport coat. He looked in his closet again, wishing he paid far more attention to those metrosexual magazines he saw at the checkout stands and a lot less attention to the California Lawyer monthly journal.

Scrutinizing himself in the full-length mirror, Ryan decided that beauty was in the eye of the beholder. He wanted people to judge him for who he was on the inside. He laughed. There were two clichés that did not jibe with looks-obsessed L.A. He just hoped that his date was not as shallow as most of the women he had met in the last few years. If she was, it would be an early night.

He grabbed his car keys from the kitchen counter and ran his hand through his hair one last time, trying not to look at the empty dog crate still assembled in his dining room. It was time to forget Sunflower and Sasha. Most of his life wishes had come true—he'd overcome his hard-scrabble background, and he had graduated from a prestigious law school. It was tempting fate to think he could have a woman just because he wanted her. Unlike his other successes, dating was a two way street. That's why he was going out with Holly Prentice tonight. She had given an unqualified "yes" when he'd asked her out, no playing around, no games. Holly worked in marketing and community development in the vast world of Equia studios where he worked as an in-house labor attorney.

Equia Children's Entertainment, quickly approaching its centennial, was one of the most well-known animation studios in Los Angeles. Its Otto the Otter trademark was almost as recognizable as Mickey Mouse. Ryan had met Holly when he had done some work on an insurance contract she needed for a volunteer event.

He had run into her on the lot occasionally after that. It was nice seeing a friendly face among the thousands of employees he saw each day. And if they both had a few free minutes, they would grab a coffee in the commissary. Since sitting at home, racking his brain as to why Sunflower would not date him was not getting him anywhere, he hoped a date with Holly, who was smart, funny and definitely pretty would break the hold Sunflower had on his heart.

The woman who answered the door was worlds apart from the woman he knew from work. Holly was wearing a tiny bronze dress that left little to the imagination and some kind of sparkly cream that made her skin glow. All that exposed leg and curly hair was wrapped up in a woman that was just his type.

Despite all that, he just wasn't that into her. He worked to hide his disinterest, hoping he wasn't too transparent. He made sure he kept up his side of the conversation while they drove to the appropriately trendy restaurant, and ordered the right wine and two of the celebrity chef's specials.

Holly sipped from her wineglass and pushed around her uneaten dinner.

"Hey there," she said softly, stopping him in the middle of a sentence. "I can see this isn't going anywhere between us. What's really on your mind tonight?"

Ryan closed his blue eyes briefly. "I met someone."

Holly's release of breath was audible. "That's such a weight off my shoulders. I met someone too. Well not exactly someone new, but I'm sort of involved with someone I've known for a long time, though I don't think I want to be… " She trailed off, seeming a little embarrassed by her candidness. "What about you?"

"I met this woman that I can't get out of my mind."

"What's she like?"

"She's nothing like me. She's a breath of fresh air. I met her in the craziest way. We were trying to save this dog on the freeway—"

Holly interrupted before he could finish his thought. "Wait. Are you talking about Sophie? My best friend, Sophie Reid?" She was suddenly more animated than she had been anytime that night.

"I didn't exactly get her name."

"But… Well, how would you describe her?"

"She's about five foot three or four with yellow, no, now I think it's purple, hair and a sunflower yellow Volkswagen Beetle with this clever vanity plate… "

"EW A BUG," they said together, laughing.

"That's definitely Sophie," she said, pausing uncertainly. "Are you guys—um—seeing each other?" she asked politely, though it was obvious from the sudden change in her demeanor that she already knew the answer.

"She won't see me," he said soberly. "But I'm pretty sure that there's something there between us. I mean, on the surface we don't have much in common, but it's like we're meant to be together."

"Mmmm, she doesn't date lawyers, you know," Holly said. "It's kind of like a bright line rule with her."

"Why?" he asked, hoping Sophie's best friend could shed some light on what he considered an unreasonable prohibition.

"I don't feel comfortable disclosing that," Holly said, clamming up. Clearly, she was in the "girls' club." He'd be lucky if he got one more morsel of information out of her tonight. "That's something she should explain to you herself, I think."

"I don't exactly know how to contact her," Ryan said, putting on the lost little boy look that most women couldn't help but find endearing. "Can you give me her number at least, so I can have that conversation with her?"

But Holly didn't seem the least bit affected by his plea. "I'm sorry, I thought I heard someone's voice," Holly said, looking over to the crowded three-deep bar, distracted for a long moment. She turned back to the table. "Ryan, I don't think I'd feel comfortable going against her wishes like that," Holly said, clearly preoccupied, looking over her other shoulder now. She turned back to their conversation again, but she had lost her earlier enthusiasm. "I can tell you that she's helping me do some volunteer work at the Korby Center next weekend."

"The Korby Center?"

"You know how I organize volunteer events for Equia, right? Well, I've had a little problem getting volunteers for this thing we're doing next weekend. We're supposed to landscape and redecorate a residential home for foster kids who've aged out of the system."

"Oh, I saw that in last month's Otter newsletter. It seemed like a worthwhile cause. I'm surprised more people from work didn't volunteer."

"Well, it's not too late to add yourself to that list. We can always use more volunteers. Plus, I guarantee Sophie will be there."

He nodded, smiling once again. "I'd love to help you out."

Holly chuckled. "I'm sure the Korby kids will appreciate your altruism." She looked over her shoulder again. "I'll, uh, e-mail you the details." She looked at his crisp tailored clothes. "Oh, and you should dress down...way down."

They took a few minutes to finish up their coffees, and had just stood, ready to go, when a dark haired man strode over purposefully.

"Crap, Ryan. It's Nick, that guy I'm sort of seeing." Her speech grew hurried. "If I don't get to say it later, thanks for the evening, it's been great. I'll keep my fingers crossed for you and Sophie. I think you'll be good for her."

"Can we talk for just a second?" the Nick guy asked brusquely. He cast a quick disapproving glance at Ryan. "Alone."

Sensing that the conversation Nick and Holly were

about to have was for their ears only, Ryan took that opportunity to step away. "I'll just arrange things with the valet. See you outside, Holly."

When Ryan came back to take Holly home, it was clear that she and Nick were in their own universe and didn't look for the world like they needed to be disturbed. But he wanted to make sure she was okay with that. It was the right thing to do.

As he approached, he heard her say, "I owe it to him to see this night through."

Ryan cleared his throat. Nick dropped his hands and stepped back from Holly, their intense stare broken.

"Holly, you don't owe me a thing. I had a very nice time with you tonight, but it looks like you have your hands full. So if everything's okay here... " She gave a reassuring nod. "I'll see you at work sometime." To Nick, he said, "You're a really lucky guy. Make sure you get her home safely."

With that, he turned on his heel and headed toward the line of shiny late model cars the valets had lined up for the patrons leaving the restaurant and got in to his Acura, smiling. Whether it was God, karma, kismet, or fate, Ryan would not look a gift horse in the mouth. People were right when they compared the entertainment industry in Los Angeles to high school. It was the most intimate circle of people. And it had led him straight to Sophie. Sure, the date hadn't gone well. It had been a freaking disaster. Nonetheless, he grinned like a fool the whole way home. By the time he met Sophie next weekend—He rolled the name around. Sophie. It suited her—he'd be ready, with a plan.

FOUR

SOPHIE STARED into the rainbow-hued jumble that was her closet. What in the heck was she gonna wear today? That was the question of the seven o'clock hour. There was nothing the least bit subtle or understated about her clothing—or her life for that matter. She would probably never admit it to her friends, and never to her family even under the threat of death, but a small but growing part of her was tired of all the bright, attention-getting outfits and outrageous colored hair. Wrapped in a gray silk kimono that matched her eyes perfectly, she wondered if her friends would recognize her if she came to the Equia volunteer event in a plain white Gap t-shirt and jeans. Probably not.

The multicolored hair, multiple piercings, and atten- tion-grabbing garments which made up Sophie's signature style had started in high school. She'd begun coloring her strawberry blonde hair because she'd always hated the color, and it was easier to color her hair in bright hues than continue to live with the perpetual teasing that befell redheads. The other accouterments—the piercings and the tight, bright clothes—had started as a rebellion against her parents and her conservative upbringing. Her parents never acknowledged her artistic talents and belittled her achievements. Selena's perfect grades were the stuff of family legend. It's what made her parents proud. Although she hadn't realized it then, she'd desperately wanted their attention and if she couldn't get it for the positive things she did, then the fourth or fifth earring and purple hair at her sister's prep school graduation surely did.

Resigning herself to her chosen fate, Sophie pulled out multi-hued blue tie dyed overalls and a sports bra. She laid the clothing on the bed then rummaged through her jars of temporary hair dye that lined a small shelf in her closet until she came upon royal blue. If a change was in order, today was probably not the day to go cold turkey.

She let Sasha out and made sure her neighbors could check on and feed her if she got back later than the dog's dinnertime. When Nick's father Dominic pulled up in his white pick-up truck, Sophie jumped in, ready to get on with the day. Now that Holly was dating Nick, she didn't feel bad taking advantage of his father's generosity. She'd known Nick since he got to L.A., and Dominic was always offering to help "the kids"—as he called them. Now that they were practically family—she let him help.

"Well, you give new meaning to idea of a blue-haired lady," Dominic said, chuckling.

"Thanks for carpooling with me," she said, ignoring the friendly jibe. "You know your way around the L.A.

area better than anyone I know. There's no reason for me to get lost trying to find this Korby Center."

"For you, pretty girl, it's no problem," he said, winking at her, and then returned his eyes to the road.

Sophie had never been good at accepting compliments. Deep in her heart, she simply didn't believe that anyone could mean them. Her mother had been stunning when she was younger. Selie was pretty, downright beautiful if she made any effort at it. Sophie had always been the plain one. Her gray eyes weren't the brilliant blue of her mother and sister. Her hair, which had been the bane of her existence as a child, had dulled from a frightening carroty orange to what she thought was a nondescript reddish blond. And while she knew that the rest of her features wouldn't scare off children at Halloween, they were, in her opinion, nothing special. Certainly, no man she'd dated had ever said so.

Dominic knew all the shortcuts and they made it to the Korby Center in Compton with time to spare. Even though Sophie's best friend Holly arranged a number of volunteer events for Equia, one of L.A.'s largest companies, she was occasionally shorthanded, especially when the projects were in the less desirable areas of town. Sophie was always available to lend a hand for a good cause and to help her friend.

Sophie was in the center's recreation room, bent double, rolling up her pant leg and tightening the fraying laces on her ancient Chuck Taylor's, when she heard the man speak.

"Well good morning to you, Ms. Sophie Reid," he said.

She looked up, startled to see Ryan. "How did you find out my name?" she asked ungraciously. Her mother would have been apoplectic at her horrible manners.

Holly, who had just walked into the room to drop off paint and supplies, tut-tutted Sophie. "Don't be so rude, hon. I didn't think your name was a state secret. It just so happens that Ryan and I both work at Equia. He mentioned saving a red dog with a yellow haired woman and I just knew it was you in all your rainbow glory. It was funny though," she said with a quick grin, "he didn't seem to have any idea what your name was. Imagine that?" Holly left the room as quickly as she had entered, and Sophie and Ryan were completely alone for the first time since she had run from his house, proverbial tail between her legs.

"Ha, ha, Holly," Sophie grumbled to her friend's retreating back. "Good morning to you too, Mister Ryan Becker," she said, continuing to crouch down to tend to the other shoe. She desperately hoped he couldn't see how her hands suddenly trembled.

She took in quiet, measured breaths attempting to control her heart rate. Even though she had glanced up at him only a second, his image had burned in her mind. She knew without looking that his jeans and t-shirt molded deliciously to his body, though they looked as if he had just stolen them from a perfectly formed mannequin. Even like this, weeks later, he still had the ability to take her breath away. In the scant two weeks she had not seen him, she'd almost been able to convince herself that the kisses they'd shared had been fortuitous, that their electric connection had been a figment of her overactive imagination.

Ryan offered his hand to help her stand when she finished tying her shoe. She grasped his strong fingers reluctantly. Touching him was like putting her hand to fire. How could she have not remembered the flame that burned between them? She instinctively pulled her hand back and, a little unstable, she lost her balance, tipping and landing against his broad muscular chest. She straightened up, but their bodies were still joined, breast to hip. Losing her balance felt like a metaphor of their relationship up until now. When she was around him, she felt unbalanced. She looked up at him and knew that her feelings showed on her face.

As Sophie got her bearings, her awareness of Ryan increased in proportion to the sudden hardness of his erection that swelled against her stomach. Afraid that she had shown too much vulnerability in that brief moment, Sophie's quickly slid her public mask back in place. Miming a cigar between her fingers, she put on her best Groucho Marx voice. "Is that a banana in your pocket, or are you just happy to see me?"

He tipped her chin up and looked into her eyes. "I think we'll need to finish this later," he said, then kissed her somewhat chastely on the lips, probably sensitive to the fact that one of the young residents could come in at any time. Her breathing accelerated, her arousal quickly matching his. The tips of her breasts felt like they were on fire even through the thick layers of her sports bra and overalls.

Holly popped her head back into the room at just the wrong moment. She slapped her free hand over her eyes dramatically. "I'm not seeing anything. Just make sure the residents don't either," she said, sounding a little school-marms. Sophie knew that she was in the wrong and decided it was probably unwise to comment on her friend's prudish tone just now. Holly peeked between her now separated fingers.

"Ryan, why don't you help me unload the trees and plants from the delivery truck?"

"I'll be with you in just one second," Ryan said, though his gaze never broke from Sophie's. Looking down, he cautiously put a few inches between him and Sophie.

"We're not even close to done here, Ms. Sophie Reid," he whispered. After he adjusted what needed adjusting, he followed Holly from the room.

With all the volunteers accounted for by nine thirty, Holly pulled out a very efficient looking clipboard and delegated duties. The kids from the center and those Nick had invited from a charter school he was involved with were assigned to yard duty, removing the dead and dying brush and planting donated plants and saplings. Whether it was a blessing or curse Sophie didn't yet know, but she was assigned to painting duty with Dominic, Nick, Ryan, and Holly. She was glad there wasn't much time to talk that morning.

They spread out drop cloths in the rooms to be painted and covered up the few pieces of remaining furniture. Dominic, who was semi-retired from dozens of years as a general contractor, gave them a quick yet thorough lesson in painting with rollers, and they got to work. Starting in one of the girls' rooms, Dominic painted the edges of the ceiling, cutting in the corners. Sophie and Holly, working together, filled in the ceilings with the sparkling white paint. Nick, Ryan, and another volunteer started in another area of the house.

By the second bedroom, they'd established a good rhythm.

"I think you should give him a chance," Holly said, pausing her back and forth movement and resting the roller in the paint tray.

"I can't believe you told him who I was and invited him here," she mumbled.

"I didn't think you'd mind this much," Holly confessed.

"But you know I don't date lawyers. That I don't date at all, really." Sophie paused, pushing the paint roller through the paint, watching the thick white liquid oozing under the applicator. "And you know damn well why," she murmured.

"He's a really nice guy who I think is interested in you for you, not because you're a novelty or because you're the judge's daughter."

"Maybe you should be taking your own advice. You've known Nick for years, but won't consider a *real* relationship with him because he doesn't have a couch?" she countered.

"Look, you may be right. But that's an issue for another day. I won't let you change the subject on me." Holly gave up the pretense of painting and sat cross-legged on the drop cloth. Sophie joined her, resting the pole of the roller on the floor. "You know I rarely give advice and don't butt into other people's business. My grandmother taught me better. But I love you like a sister, and I want you to be happy."

"But I am happy," Sophie countered. "I love my job. I have great friends. And I've just adopted the most wonderful puppy."

"Okay, I'll agree that your life is just dandy. Great sex can put icing on that cake."

Sophie stared intently at her pant cuffs.

Dominic poked his head in the room. "You gals would never survive on a job site," he tsked. "Trust women to get into a hen session." He waved his hand in an upward sweeping motion. "I've cut in the last bedroom. C'mon and fill that in. Then we can get started on the walls."

Sophie stood up quickly, kicked her high-tops together, and gestured in a mock salute to Dominic. "Yes, sir. We're on it, sir."

Holly laughed. They all knew Dominic was a softy under the gruff, mock-sexist exterior. Dominic walked back across the hall, Holly gathered up the paint, and Sophie carefully carried the rollers, trying to prevent any drips. When they set everything down in the final bedroom, Sophie broke the silence.

"I'll think about what you said. Seriously, I promise," she said, solemnly crossing her heart with her right index finger. "It's just that I don't think Ryan will wave some magic wand and set my inner sex pot free." Though she liked the feel of his wand.

They quickly painted the last ceiling and gathered in

the recreation room, where the guys were almost done painting the periwinkle blue walls. Sophie couldn't help notice that Ryan's hair was damp against the nape of his neck and his muscles bunched with effort. The crowded room helped her fight her urge to touch him.

Holly assigned a couple of kids to wash their paint supplies in the utility room. She set out some mini bagels, cream cheese, and orange juice, inviting everyone in for a quick mid-morning break. Sophie, who was usually in the middle of any fray, sat off to the side, thoughtfully chewing her tiny bagel. Dominic, who never missed an opportunity to eat, sat beside her on the tarp-covered couch.

"It's been a long time since I saw you, girlie. How are you?" In the past, Sophie had seen Dominic a lot more often. Holly was known for her large holiday gatherings and Nick and his dad had stopped by a lot when Nick had been working for Holly's ex-husband. Dominic had always seen through Sophie's tough-girl façade and they had taken a liking to each other. He continued before she could answer. "It looks like you've got a new hole in your ear since the last time I saw you."

Sophie fingered the last of the hoops along the shell of her left ear. "It's probably the last one. I think they hurt more the older you get."

"I hear that you're giving that guy Ryan over there a hard time," he said, gesturing toward the men laughing in the corner of the room.

"Aw, Dominic, not you too," Sophie cried in mock surrender. "I give up."

"You girls are so hard on nice guys these days. First

Holly, and now you. What does a guy have to do to get a girl interested?"

"I can't speak for Holly," Sophie said, "but dating's hard in the new millennium."

"What's so hard? My Iris and I never had all these problems," he said, referring to his now deceased wife. "You liked the way a girl looked, you asked her out. You saw a movie, had a hamburger, and talked. If you liked each other, you did it again. If not, you did it again with another person until you got it right."

"Dominic, I wish it were that easy."

Nick's father harrumphed loudly. "I think you all make it too complicated," he grumbled. "I talked to the guy this morning. He seems nice. He has a job. He doesn't smell."

Before Sophie could think of a witty or at least logical rejoinder, Holly was clapping her hands together getting the group's attention. She redirected the kids to new gardening tasks and turned organization of the painting over to Dominic.

"Last time I checked, there was too much talking and not enough painting gettin' done," Dominic said, looking pointedly from Sophie to Holly. "So I'm changing things up. Holly, you and Nick are painting the pink and green rooms, and I'll work with Sophie and Ryan to get the purple and blue-green rooms done. Hopefully we'll be dry enough in time for the afternoon furniture deliveries."

Sophie knew a setup when she saw one. First Holly, now Dominic. They were pushing her and Ryan together, and her rebellious nature made her want to push back. Not because she wasn't attracted to him—it was getting very hard to ignore her attraction to him when they were in the same room together. But because it was starting to feel like a setup by a well-meaning mother or aunt. And Sophie knew how to handle those. First, she thanked them. Then, she made a date for drinks at a loud restaurant far from her house. And lastly if she could, she went by another name. Obligation fulfilled, she never saw the guy again.

Thank goodness Dominic was there to act as a buffer. If she could just get through today, then she could have time to think about what Dominic and Holly had said and decide if she was ready to act on her feelings.

The three of them worked in relative quiet, painting the first bedroom a soft lilac. Dominic was suspiciously efficient, and had painted the room's edges and corners expertly.

"I gotta check on Nicky." He paused meaningfully. "So...I'll leave you guys to fill in these walls here." And with that he nimbly—quite nimbly for an older man—sprinted from the room.

"Well, that was subtle," Ryan said, laughing.

Sophie shook her head ruefully. "What exactly did you say to him this morning?" she asked. "He took a liking to you kind of quickly. I think he practically has us walking down the aisle." She hummed Mendelssohn's "Wedding March" under her breath.

"I told him the truth," he said.

Sophie's stomach bottomed out. He liked her, he really liked her. Damn it, she sounded like Sally Field. She felt lighthearted and joyous all at once. Here she was, the blue-haired Goth girl, and this hot guy with beautiful blue eyes and thick leonine hair wanted to kiss her. She could scarcely believe it. As they finished the last wall, she glanced surreptitiously at the broad expanse of his back, the narrow hips, the perfect muscular butt, and her breath quickened, and her mouth watered. Maybe she could give it a whirl with him. Maybe this time it would be different. They weren't getting married—she didn't believe in marriage—so maybe she could break her rule if a quick romp with this guy was in the cards.

He completed the last bare spot on the plaster surface and set down his roller. Sophie picked up her supplies. "We only have one room left before lunch," she said innocently, then sashayed from the room, swinging her hips provocatively in a way she was sure would grab his attention.

She heard him drop something and curse swiftly under his breath. But he was with her in the corner room in a matter of moments. Dominic had completed the preliminary work on this room as well. She guessed they'd have a few moments alone. When she pushed the heavy door with her foot, it closed with a click that echoed in the empty room. In seconds, she closed the distance between them and snaked her arms around his waist, pushing up his white t-shirt, and kissed him hard. Her last thought was to remember to thank Holly for insisting they use low odor paint. The only risk of suffocation was if she and Ryan didn't come up for air soon enough.

SOPHIE HAD MORE switchbacks than Coldwater Canyon. One moment she was as hot as molten wax, another, as cold as stone. As Sophie thrust her tongue in his mouth and ran her short nails down his bare back, Ryan decided he preferred her hot. He cupped her sweet little bottom and molded her against his erection. The friction felt so good, he didn't want to finish painting or do any more volunteer work. He wanted her in his bed, underneath him right now. But years of delayed gratification had taught him that some things were worth waiting for. Reluctantly, he broke contact with her.

"I think we better get started..." He paused to take in a shuddered breath and she lifted a pierced eyebrow suggestively. "...painting this room before we wreck Dominic's work."

In silence humming with sexual tension, they poured the evergreen paint into a large tray and dipped their rollers. Sophie started at the far corner of one wall. Peeking over her shoulder and looking unabashedly at his package, she smiled. "I guess you were happy to see me."

"You could say that," he choked out, mentally dousing himself in the coldest water he could imagine—a January swim off the Malibu coast without a wetsuit.

They both started when a tentative knock sounded at the door. Sophie, done with her wall, pulled the door open to admit Holly.

"We just closed it to making painting above the doorway easier," Sophie offered guiltily.

Holly studiously ignored their excuses. "Lunch is ready when you guys are. The caterers have set up everything." She left the room as quickly as she had entered.

Sobered, they made quick work of the remaining unpainted areas and cleaned up their equipment. Ryan made sure he wasn't alone with Sophie the rest of the afternoon. Something about her made him rush in, throwing common sense to the wind. He did everything he could to exhaust himself—moving heavy furniture, helping place a burlap wrapped tree ball in the ground. He heaved mattresses in place, and set up donated computer equipment.

Though he had initially come to Korby to corner Sophie, he was glad he had volunteered. He learned a lot about what good work the center did helping kids who didn't have anyone else to help them. He even made a note in his Blackberry, when no one was looking, to send them a donation when he got home. Equia had done a lot today, but the center could use all the help it could get.

He had cleaned up the best he could in the utility sink, but he lingered looking around for Sophie.

She popped out onto the front lawn and came to stand beside him. "Suddenly Dominic has to run a million errands tonight." She linked her paint-splattered elbow with this. "Think you can give me a ride up to the Valley?"

He tipped an imaginary hat. "It would be my pleasure."

SOPHIE KISSED and hugged her friends and slipped into the Acura.

As Ryan was about to pull out of the small parking lot, she gasped, and he slammed his foot on the brake throwing them against the seatbelts.

"What is it? You okay?" he asked, concerned.

"I think I got paint on your nice leather seats," she explained.

He breathed an audible sigh of relief. "It's only a car. Just don't let anything happen to the woman in that seat."

Sophie was surprised that Ryan didn't need directions to her Studio City home on Babcock Avenue. Most Angelenos were unable to picture the San Fernando Valley as anything but one giant unhip, monolithic suburb.

Sophie lost a little bit of her bravado for every mile they got closer to her house. Once he got to her house he'd have certain expectations that she suspected she couldn't fulfill. "You seem to know your way around the Valley," she said into the silence of the car just to have something to say.

"I grew up here," he said.

"Really? Where?" she asked, unable to hide the surprise in her voice. "I've lived around Studio City and North Hollywood for years."

"Near Victory and White Oak," he said, elaborating no further.

He was from the hot center of the Valley that walked the often-unstable line between working and middle class. The 'Beverly Hills Post Office' house and tailored button-down wardrobe did not bring Reseda to mind. Sophie refrained from asking the follow up questions that sprang to her lips. That kind of conversation would reveal more about herself than she was willing.

Ryan's large hand set the parking brake as he pulled up to her house and brought her mind back to the issue at hand.

This was where it always got hairy for her. She had no idea how to get them from point A—fully clothed—to point B—hot, sweaty, and naked on her crisp white sheets. And she wanted to get there—bad. She invited Ryan into the house and left him to wander as she let Sasha out. It was going to take a lot of Dutch courage to get through tonight—but if their earlier kisses were any indication—this time it would be worth it.

FIVE

"SO WHAT'S your real hair color, if I may ask?"

Sophie took a gulp from one of the large glasses of wine she had poured for herself and Ryan. "So formal," she said, her voice dropping a register. "Yes, you may ask if the drapes match the carpet. Isn't that what you really want to know?"

A slight blush rose high on Ryan's cheekbones. She was sure he did not usually hear that kind of language in his ivory tower universe.

"You're not going to shock me out of being attracted to you," he said matter-of-factly. "I think you're cute with blue or pink or yellow hair. I was just wondering where you started."

Discombobulated by her second compliment of the day, she took another greedy swallow of wine, and poured more into her glass from the now half-empty bottle on the coffee table.

Ryan carefully placed his own goblet on the wood. "Do I scare you?" he asked, looking directly into her eyes.

Sophie's eyes skidded away from Ryan's intense azure gaze. She looked at the dog, hoping for salvation from her sudden feelings for Ryan. The damned cur was no help. She was sound asleep, snoring audibly, feet twitching in the way only dogs in REM sleep do. She'd love it if the dog's need to go to the bathroom would excuse her from this conversation. Sophie considered nudging Sasha with her bare foot, but that would be too obvious. Instead, she filled her wine glass to the brim and scooted to the far corner of the room's only seating, taking her wine with her. She wished right then that she'd had the money to buy a chair for the room as well, so she could be far enough away that the citrusy scent emanating from him didn't make her swoon.

After that long delay, she answered untruthfully. "No." Then she took another sip of wine. She held the glass's stem tight in a death grip.

Ryan eased back into the sofa's other corner and crossed one long leg across the other knee. Looking like he had settled in for the long haul, he examined her thoughtfully.

"Why don't you date lawyers?" he asked. When she did not answer right away, he continued. "I want to know because *I* want to…date you." But from his tone it sounded like he had far more in mind than just *dating*.

"But you don't know me," Sophie said, deflecting the question. "From what I can see, I can't be your usual type."

Ryan smiled at that. "You're right. I usually date boring women with boring jobs who want three kids and a pseudo Mediterranean McMansion. You're none of those things. You're bold, funny, brash, interesting, and pretty. I'm a guy so I'll admit that part of my attraction to you is purely physical. I haven't been able to look at another woman since I met you."

Sophie laughed, something she'd never done during or leading up to sex with someone. Maybe it was going to be okay.

"This is a modern miracle," she proclaimed. "A guy who doesn't look. Call Oprah and Barbara Walters! Forget that. Call NBC. You'll be on *Dateline*." She was practically shouting, causing Sasha to open one sleepy eye cautiously.

"Okay, maybe I still look," Ryan said, backing off good-naturedly. "I am a guy. But the only woman I think about being with is you," he said seriously. Sophie's laughter ceased abruptly.

She started getting the jittery feeling in her stomach that she got when a man was going to try to kiss her. She hated herself for constantly feeling like a teenager around attractive members of the opposite sex no matter how old she was. She took another sip of wine, and noticed that at least she had started feeling the calming effects of the alcohol. *Thank goodness*, she thought.

"I have blue hair," Sophie said, trying to delay what she knew was coming. Did all guys get that seriously sexy intense look before they were going to pounce on a girl?

Ryan didn't exactly pounce. Instead, his movements were slow and deliberate, giving her time to back out. She very much didn't want to back out. But there was no mistaking his intention. He unwrapped her fingers from her now half-empty wine glass, and put it on the small coffee table.

"Sunflower, you're the funniest, most spontaneous person I've ever met," he said, stroking her blue bangs. "I want to finish what we started this morning." Then he kissed her. It had been a long time since Sophie had deliberately kissed a man, and she couldn't ever remember being kissed like this. It was very different from their earlier spontaneous encounters.

Though it was only his lips that grazed hers, Sophie could feel Ryan everywhere, from her tingling nipples to her pulsing sex. The pressure from his lips made her fingers itch to touch him. The room suddenly felt twenty degrees warmer than it had moments before.

One of Ryan's hands slid from her hair and gently traced the shell of her ear, stopping at each ring that studded the rim, and the other moved from her shoulder to her hip. She held her breath. It was going okay so far. It felt good. Then she tensed when his hands caressed the small of her back through the open side vent of the overalls.

He pulled his mouth from hers and placed soothing kisses on her forehead, her studded eyebrow, on the delicate skin of her eyelids. The room had gotten dark as dusk fell and the autumn sun had set. Other than the firm line of his stubbled jaw and blue eyes now almost black with desire, twilight obscured most of his features. From what she could see, though, confusion warred with desire on his handsome face.

He thrust his hands into his hair, making the waves almost stand on end. "I want to make love with you in the worst way, Sophie." He blew out a breath. "But I'm getting mixed signals here. Do you want to be with me? Now?" Ryan asked, his voice rough with need and slightly tinged with the fear of rejection.

Alcohol fueling her bravado, Sophie nodded in silent response. She grasped Ryan's hand and all but dragged him to her bedroom before she lost her nerve. The only light in the sparsely furnished room came from a long horizontal window over the bed and a low wattage fixture near the closet. Brightly colored Indian print scarves tented the overhead light, as well as her bedside lamps. She turned on the lights, throwing the area into stark red relief. The reds and purples set the scene for seduction.

She expected him to kiss her again, needing him to take charge. Sophie wanted to lose herself in that kiss's potential. It would be one hundred times easier than having to think about what she was doing and with whom. Most people were carried away during sex. At least, that's the way the steamy erotic novels she sometimes read portrayed it. With the two men she had ever been with, she was awkwardly self-conscious during the entire act, and it was happening again. She hadn't drank enough to slip into obliviousness.

Instead of kissing her, Ryan surprised her by slowly unlatching the hooks of the overalls and allowing the bib and straps to fall from her body to a blue heap on the floor. She stepped from the pool of tie dyed cotton, clad only in her sports bra and discount store white cotton briefs that covered everything and left a whole lot to the imagination. If Ryan noticed the incongruity between her undergarments and the loud, revealing clothes she usually wore, he didn't say a thing.

"You okay, Sunflower?" Ryan asked, gently pushing her blue hair away from her face.

Sophie nodded and hesitantly reached out to touch him. She stroked his fine, silky hair, traced her finger down his corded neck, and ran her hands lightly down the back of his shirt feeling his muscles bunch slightly at her touch. It floored her that she could get this kind of reaction from him.

"I think you have too many clothes on," she whispered in the deepening darkness.

Faster than the blink of an eye, Ryan was out of his t-shirt and jeans. He dropped a condom onto the wrinkled bedcovers.

"Sure of yourself, huh?" Sophie whispered, very thankful that she didn't have to reveal the seventy-two pack of condoms in her bedside drawer—or the fact that the box was hermetically sealed in its original cellophane.

"Just hopeful," he said. "Very hopeful." In the dim light of the closet bulb, she could see his erection barely jutting from the open placket of his underwear. He wore boxers. She should have guessed. Ryan seemed like a starched cotton boxer kind of guy. He pulled her closer so they were mostly skin-to-skin and kissed her. Finally. Any thoughts of underwear choice left her mind.

He teased her lips with his, at first hesitant, then with growing pressure as she leaned into him more heavily. As he sought and gained access with his tongue, she ran her hands along his smooth back and muscular arms. It felt like heaven, being held by him. It had been so long since she had shared a good kiss with a man, the kind that made her tingle everywhere. Ryan pulled her even closer and his hands strayed to her briefs. He slipped his warm palms under the elastic waist and cupped her small round bottom, bringing her into close contact with his penis, which bobbed gently as if beckoning her.

Ryan eased the panties from her thighs, shucked his own undergarments, and left them in a pool on the floor with their other clothes. He pulled her gently to lie down on the slightly mussed bedcovers, deftly sliding the condom under a pillow. "I think it's you who has on too many clothes now." He gingerly eased the tight-fitting blue elastic bra over her breasts and head, leaving them both bare from head to toe. Reflexively, Sophie moved her arms across her breasts.

"You're beautiful. There's no need to hide yourself from me," Ryan said, lifting her arm away from her chest.

Sophie's face warmed and she was glad that he couldn't see her blush in the darkness. "But I take after my father, up top. My boobs are too small and my nipples too large..." she said, trailing off.

Ryan laughed. He propped up on an elbow staring down at her. "In negotiation there's something called not talking after the close." He smoothed his hand along her collarbone, down her thin arm, and captured her small hand in his. "I'm here because I want to be here and I'm very attracted to you. You are not going to be able to talk me out of wanting you, Sophie. I've been thinking about this far too long for that to happen."

When his head came closer she felt her body vibrate, waiting for one of those bone melting kisses, but was taken aback when he kissed her breasts, his lips teasing everywhere with little butterfly kisses before taking one dusky nipple then the other deep into his warm mouth. When she thought she would not be able to take any more, Ryan's fingers smoothed over her slightly convex stomach and parted her nether lips below. He slowly stroked her clit already slick with her arousal. It went on like that, Ryan alternating between lavishing attention on both breasts and sipping at her lips as if she were the finest champagne.

Her arms felt like dead fish at her sides. It was times like this her inexperience showed. Should she touch him —touch him there—where men most craved? Unsure, she tentatively stroked his hair again, the curve of his jaw, retracing ground that was now becoming familiar. She skated her hand down his arm, marveling at the springy hairs that gently tickled the pads of her fingers. More uncertain than ever, she stroked his hip.

Only when he paused in his own ministrations, expectant, did she touch the soft skin of his erection. It jumped of its own accord, seeming to enjoy the tactile stimulation. Emboldened, if only slightly, she traced the contours of his penis with her fingertips. It was like smooth velvet over hardened steel. Ryan pulled her away from his organ and grasped her hand and intertwined their fingers. "Can we...are you ready?"

Sophie nodded, still mute. Ryan found the condom under her head and sheathed himself. He rose over her, bracing his forearms on both sides of her head and kissed her deeply, easing her legs apart with one knee. He made sure she was ready for him and guided himself toward her center. She gasped, tensing when he was only in halfway.

SOPHIE'S BODY gripped him like a fist. He didn't know if he would be able to last long like this. He liked to pride himself on making it a good experience for the woman he was with, and didn't want his first time—or any time—with Sophie to be a quick wham bam. He tried to slow his breathing. "You okay?" he asked when he regained the ability to speak.

"I'm okay," she let out with a hiss, releasing the breath she had been holding. "I just need you to go slow."

Ryan pulled out almost the entire way. Then, holding himself as steady as possible, he eased his cock back in and out several times very slowly, a little farther each time, until he'd buried himself up to the root. He blew out a breath, closed his eyes, and turned his head. Ryan tried to think about baseball, politics, or anything that wouldn't excite him. He didn't want to slam into her as if he was a piston rod that could not stop.

When he was back under control again, he began to move slowly, insinuating his hand between them and caressing the small nubbin that he knew would bring her pleasure. Whether it was two minutes or twenty, he couldn't say, but while Sophie's breathing quickened and her nipples were hard, he didn't think she was any closer to an orgasm than she had been minutes ago. He strongly believed in "ladies first," but knew he could not endure the mind-bending pleasure of being inside her much longer.

"Sophie." He paused mid stroke, looking down at her

closed eyes. Her serene face revealed nothing. "I can't hold out much longer." It had been a long time for him and his body was ready to go no matter what his brain wanted or she needed. "Oh, God," he breathed. "I promise to make you feel this good." The next downward stroke obliterated any coherent thought. It all boiled down to sensation for Ryan. When it came, his orgasm was deep and long.

Concern tinged the glow of pleasure when reality surfaced. He came back from a quick trip to the bathroom to take care of essentials and laid down next to her on the cool cotton sheet.

Ryan pulled the thin summer blanket over their bodies. "Sophie, I'm sorry about that, but I promise there won't be a repeat performance." He caressed her arm, bare above the covers, and then slowly pulled the cover from her breasts, feeling himself harden just looking at her. She made him feel like he was twenty all over again.

She pulled the covers back up, covering herself, and halting his roaming hands. "It's okay, Ryan. I don't…" Unexpectedly, she darted from the bed and pulled on a t-shirt and sweats from a shelf in the closet.

"Where are you going?"

Sophie glanced meaningfully at the combination alarm clock/compact disc player on her bedside table.

"It's past seven and Sasha has to go for her evening walk now," she said, practically dashing from the room.

She had Sasha leashed up and her running shoes laced when Ryan hopped into the room, still trying to get the second leg into his paint-splattered jeans. "I'll come with you. Just give me a moment."

Sophie looked put out waiting for Ryan, but she didn't open the front door, despite the dog's whining and licking of the doorjamb, until his shoes were properly on his feet.

Ryan hadn't paid much attention to the street when he'd been driving her home—his mind had been on other things—but he looked around now, keenly observant. He had never spent much time in this part of the San Fernando Valley, except for business meetings at the various studios.

Her street, like the one he'd grown up on, was full of small tract houses built in the postwar fifties. But that's where the similarities ended. Where his mother's street had remained the same for over fifty years, Sophie's had evolved. Developers had torn down or substantially reno-vated most of the houses. A foreign or luxury car graced every driveway.

Sophie and Sasha were off like a shot. She walked toward the Studio City Golf and Tennis Club, following the path along the back of the golf course, the dog sniffing and meandering. He watched them meander along the tree lawn for what felt like an eternity before he trotted down the sidewalk and caught up with them.

ONE DAY SOPHIE wanted to have an orgasm that she didn't initiate and complete herself. Her handheld shower-head had stood in for her boyfriend for years and she was damned tired of it. Ryan had tried, she knew he had. And it had felt good, really good, until it hadn't. She'd been right on the edge. It had been better than the past, but it just wasn't enough. She'd wanted nothing more than to let go, but it hadn't come. It never did.

Sophie heard Ryan coming up behind her. The tightness in the pit of her stomach grew. She was dreading their post-coital conversation because she knew how it was going to end. He would say they were different, that she was unusually inhibited and unresponsive, and plain just not sexy. It wasn't going to work. No matter how he put it, the bottom line was that he was leaving. They always did, sooner or later. This would be sooner than most. She took a deep breath and got ready to let him off the hook.

"You don't have to say anything. It didn't work out, but..." Sophie petered out before she could finish her speech. The older she got, the harder this was. She looked down, suddenly fascinated by the dog's every movement. Now that she had a dog, she could happily die a spinster. Why were all these old-fashioned words ringing in her head? As long as she didn't become a crazy cat lady, she thought she could live a very long and satisfying life without male companionship. Maybe she was just not meant to have a fulfilling sex life with any man. Happily ever after—or happy for now wasn't for everyone. It was time she acknowledged that and moved on.

Ryan squatted and scratched the dog behind her ears. Sasha was easy. She wagged her tail and licked his hand in response. Damn dog sold her out.

"Do you really hate sex?" he asked, looking up at her, his gorgeous face anguished. "I would never have...if I thought you were remotely serious." He raked his hand through his already mussed golden hair. "It was so good for me. I just want to make you feel as good as I did."

Ryan stood and they walked back to the house in silence. She let the dog off the leash and Sasha immediately ran to her water dish, the lapping sounds the only noise in the otherwise quiet house. The room went from darkness to light when Sophie flipped on the sole torchiere lamp. She kept moving through the house, turning on the lights in the dining room and kitchen and the family room. She kicked off her shoes and padded back to the kitchen in her bare feet, her blue toenails peeking out from under her long knit pants.

"I'm going to make something to eat. Remind me to tell Holly that bagels and sandwiches aren't enough for hard-working volunteers. You want anything or are you going home?"

"Sophie, I'm not leaving with things like this." His voice rang with distress, but when he spoke again his tone was softer. "I'll have whatever you're having."

RYAN PULLED himself up onto one of the barstools that abutted the kitchen's large pass-through, and watched Sophie gather food from the refrigerator. It looked like he was in for breakfast at dinner. He wasn't complaining.

"Are you ever going to answer me?" he asked. He stacked his elbows on the cool black granite counter and leaned on his clasped hands. She paused her chopping of tomatoes and peppers, and looked directly at him, her gray eyes coolly assessing him.

"It's your lucky day," she said, quirking one studded eyebrow. "I'll answer only one, so choose carefully."

Ryan thought carefully. There was so much he wanted to know about this complex woman. He was pretty sure that he had a good idea about her real hair color. It had been dark in her bedroom, but not that dark. He didn't think it was wise to broach the topic of lawyers. There was no reason to give her an excuse not to see him, so he decided to skip that hot button issue for now. What really bothered him was why an attractive, responsive woman like her didn't enjoy sex. So he took the plunge and asked the hardest question. "What can I do to make sex better for you?" he asked softly. "You were with me when I kissed you. I loved feeling your nipples get hard in my mouth. You got so very wet when I touched you. Why did I lose you? Did I do something you didn't like?"

The only indication that Sophie heard him was the very short pause she took while adding grated cheese to the frying eggs. She deftly flipped the omelet over and simultaneously pulled toast from the toaster. A woman's ability to multitask always amazed him. After she poured them both orange juice and buttered their white toast, she answered him.

"Nothing," she said with such finality he thought that was the end of it. She paused for a long time, immobile. "You saw what happened earlier, Ryan. It has always been like that for me. A lot of wine, a lot of awkwardness followed by the huge letdown," she said quietly. After serving up the eggs, she came around and claimed the stool next to his, avoiding his eyes.

Ryan put down his fork, his omelet forgotten for a moment. "You've never had an orgasm with a man?"

Sophie stopped eating and shifted on the stool, visibly uncomfortable with the frank discussion. "When I was younger and lost my virginity, it didn't happen, but I just chalked it up to being young and inexperienced. It never got better, though."

Ryan cursed under his breath. "What were you feeling back there when we were…?"

Sophie took a deep breath. "It's like being on a roller coaster. Your stomach does belly flops and you have this very exhilarating feeling, then nothing. The ride's over before you really begin to enjoy it."

They returned to eating. Ryan considered her words. When they were almost done, the silence was broken by the blare of a Snoop Dogg song.

"Oh, my phone," Sophie said, looking around the kitchen and dining room for the cell. "Hello," she said answering the call. "Mmmm, now? Really, at Hannah's place?" She squinted at the blue LED clock on the microwave. "Cool, I'll be over in a little bit. I'll need to… uhh…wrap up what I'm doing here, and shower. See you later, then."

Ryan didn't pretend he hadn't heard her side of the conversation. "Going out?"

Sophie's head was somewhere else, their conversation already a thing of the past. She headed into the bedroom, pulling a skimpy looking top and mini skirt from her closet along the way. When he cleared his throat, she looked up, feigning surprise that he was still there.

"You're leaving? Just like that?" he asked matter-of-factly.

"I didn't plan it this way." She pulled a towel from the bathroom door, ready to shower. "But with early calls, it's rare that all of us from work can get together at an adult hour."

Ryan needed to be alone. He needed time to think. He could not bully Sophie into being with him. A few hours with a yellow pad and he would put together a plan. Plus, he didn't think he could watch her leave the house scantily clad knowing some other horny guy was going to be looking at her. He pulled his Blackberry from his pants and turned on the electronic gadget with a beep.

"Eight one eight…" he started.

"You want my number?" She appeared genuinely incredulous. "You want to see me again?"

Ryan sighed. "Yes, Miss Sophie Reid, I would like that very much."

She dropped the towel, flustered. She quickly gave him her number and picked up the towel. "So, you'll call?" she asked in a hushed voice.

His heart melted. She was so brash on the outside, but clearly vulnerable underneath all the smoke and mirrors.

He strode across the room and kissed her hard. Ryan schooled himself not to look down at her unfettered breasts as they bobbed gently under her t-shirt. He wanted to smooth his hands along her lithe little body until she cried out in ecstasy—he was half hard thinking about ways he could bring them indescribable pleasure. Instead, he practiced restraint. He tipped up her chin and pecked her on her freckled nose. "Yes, I'll call."

. . .

SOPHIE WALKED THROUGH THE COURTYARD, past
the dry pool and empty fountain that lent Hannah's apartment building an air of faded glory. She'd had far too
much wine to drive and had walked the mile or so to the
party. Following the beat of the music, she made her way
to the door of her friend's apartment. It was slightly ajar,
and she walked right in without invitation. Though the
music was loud, the gathering was mellow. Everyone was
sitting grouped in various conversations. She was hoping
for more of a celebratory atmosphere from the impromptu
get together to help her forget about this evening's disaster. But this was cool too. Sam and Alyssa, her assistants
from her show, waved her over to their group around the
dining room table.

"What took you so long to get over here?" Alyssa
asked. Before Sophie could answer, she peppered her with
another question. "Do you want a beer?"

"I've already had too much to drink today," she said
waving away the alcoholic beverage.

"Were you drinking alone?" Alyssa asked salaciously.
She was the drama queen of the group.

"Um, not exactly," Sophie admitted, trying not to look
shifty eyed under her friends' scrutiny.

"Shit," Alyssa said, loud enough for everyone to hear.
"I think our fearless leader got laid tonight."

A whoop went up from the small group assembled at
the table. Sophie wished fervently she wasn't blushing red
to the roots of her blue hair.

"Oh my God, Alyssa's right," Sam said, observing her

very closely. "Give me the who, what, where, why, and when, honey. Dish."

"It's nothing, and whatever it was is *not* going to happen again, so we can cut the discussion right now," she said, slicing her hand across her throat.

"Why?" Sam wailed plaintively. He sounded like he'd been personally kicked to the curb.

"Long story short," Sophie started, knowing that not saying anything would yield minutes, if not hours of water torture-like interrogation from her friends. "He was a lawyer. And a lousy lay," Sophie finished, hoping she wouldn't be caught in her bald-faced lie.

The diversion worked. Sophie cringed inwardly at her public disparagement of Ryan. Since they would never meet him, it wouldn't make any difference. It was gracious of him to ask for her number, but he would never call. When she tuned back into the conversation, they were on to a new topic.

"Speaking of lawyers," Sam dished, "Have you heard the rumors? There's talk that the union's going to strike." The makeup artists and hair dressers who worked on movie and television productions were members of the International Alliance of Theatrical Stage Employees, Local 706.

But this was the first Sophie had heard of a strike. With everything else that was happening in her life, this was the last thing she needed.

SIX

ON DAY ONE, she could excuse him. It was Sunday. No one called on Sunday. He was probably doing the same things she was—cleaning the house, doing the laundry, finishing last-minute errands before the work week started. If he was anything like her father, he was probably working today as well. Lawyers never knew when to turn it off. Though she thought Ryan had a better handle on it. He didn't seem like the workaholic type.

She was pulled away from her reflection and self-pity when her ringer blared Sunday afternoon. Her disappointment that it wasn't Ryan was quickly replaced by rabid curiosity.

"Nick?" she queried, pulling away from the phone and looking at her caller ID. "What's up?" She could not remember Nick calling her in the last five years. "Is Holly okay?"

"That's kind of why I'm calling," he said. She heard a sudden crashing sound in the background as if he'd dropped the phone. "Sorry, I'm getting my luggage down for a trip to New York."

"Okay," Sophie said slowly. "What's going on with Hol?"

"Nothing major. She's kinda sick today with some flu bug or something. I think she'll be fine, but I'd sure appreciate it if you could maybe check on her."

"Of course," she said, then ended the call. She called Holly's cell, but got no answer, so she left a message wishing her friend well. Now she had two things to worry about—Holly and Ryan.

On the second day, a little niggle of doubt crept into her head. Maybe he wasn't the guy she thought he was. Maybe he was like all the others. But she could excuse Ryan for not calling on a first day of a busy workweek. Years ago, she had learned that Monday was the worst day for a job interview, because people were overwhelmed when they came back from a weekend, catching up with what was on their desks.

She called Holly again, but got the machine. Maybe there was something wrong with her karma. She put her phone in her apron, pulled out her sable brushes and got back to work.

By Tuesday, all the usual self-doubts and recriminations surfaced. Men always said they were going to call, then never did. She was old enough to know that. Getting your number was a way to end an acquaintance without having to say right out, *I'm not attracted to you. This isn't going anywhere.* Sophie felt stupid, naïve, clueless for thinking that this time was any different than the others. Guys didn't like making love to a woman as responsive as a cold fish, and definitely didn't call to see them again. There was never going to be any bathroom graffiti displaying her number for a good time.

When the line producer announced that the show was off for a few days while the kids caught up on legally required school hours, she decided to pop over to Holly's office for lunch. Maybe a little girl talk could assuage her worries about the sincerity of Ryan's interest. Holly had far more real-life experience with men than she did; after all, she'd been married.

Holly, who never missed a day of work, ever, that Sophie could remember, had called in sick. Guilt washed over Sophie like a cold shower, snapping her from her malaise. She had spent the last two days twiddling her thumbs, worrying about Ryan's rejection instead of following up on her unanswered messages. She dialed Holly's home number, determined to redeem herself.

"I stopped by your office to see if you were free for lunch. Your assistant told me you'd called in sick for the last two days. You okay?"

"Soph, I don't know." Holly paused. Her voice sounded unusually timid. "I got really sick at Nick's place. I feel like I must have some kind of weird flu or something."

"I'm coming over."

"You don't have to do that," Holly said, though it was clear from the inflection in her tone that someone coming over to care for her was exactly what she needed. "I thought you were on the set of one of the kids' shows today."

"I have a couple of days free. The young star has to

make up some missed school hours, so the crew's off." The reception cut out as Sophie got into her car. When they could hear each other again, Sophie's brain kicked into gear. "I'm going to stop at the drugstore and load up on stuff. What kind of symptoms do you have?"

Holly's voice was muffled. "It started with me barfing at Nick's place."

"Oh, that's bad," Sophie groaned. "He must really like you if he sticks around after that."

Holly ignored her friend's comment. "It feels like a bad period. Probably something we ate. I let him talk me into too much junk food on the pier with a nacho chaser."

Sophie nodded, her eyes glued to the dashboard. "Oh, okay. See you in a bit."

My God, Holly sounds like she's pregnant. Holly might suddenly be deaf, dumb, and blind to her symptoms, but Sophie wasn't. She picked up the requisite Pepto-Bismol, saltines, ginger ale, and club soda, but threw in a pastel colored box of pregnancy tests for good measure.

Unceremoniously, Sophie dumped the plastic carryout bag on the table. The contents spilled out haphazardly.

"Sophie, you're a godsend," Holly said, twisting the cap off the ginger ale and pouring herself a glass. "Wait, why did you buy that?" she said pointing at the early pregnancy test kit on the table. "I'm sick with some weird stomach flu, not pregnant."

Raising one pierced eyebrow skeptically, Sophie looked hard at Holly. "Clearly, I'm no medical expert, though I did work on a doctor show once, but you're acting a lot like my sister Selie did in her first trimester. When was your last period anyway?"

"I don't remember, but Nick and I have always used protection," she said emphatically. Then she paused. "Except…"

"Except for what?"

"Just that first time," Holly said abashedly. She winced at the memory. "We got a little carried away."

"Sounds like a lot carried away." Sophie pushed the slim pastel pink and blue box into her hands. "Just do this to be sure. Then I'll take you to Canter's and we can try the chicken soup cure."

They never got to the twenty-four hour Jewish deli or to Sophie's dilemma about Ryan, which now seemed trivial in comparison. Holly was pregnant. Sophie was no less shocked than Holly. Of course, she knew where babies came from. She just hadn't imagined that her very responsible friend could be so careless. She winced thinking back to Saturday night with Ryan. She'd been so self-conscious of her body, of the sex act itself, that pulling out her unused box of condoms would have been mortifying. But seeing Holly overwhelmed by an unplanned pregnancy convinced Sophie that she'd have to get over her embarrassment and take charge of protecting herself—that was, if she ever got the chance again.

RYAN PICKED at the Cobb salad his assistant Evangeline had brought. Healthy eating was one thing, but sometimes he just wanted real food for lunch. Shoving more eggs, bacon, and avocado into his mouth, and ignoring all that lettuce, he worried over the pages of notes he'd made on a yellow legal pad. In bold print at the top of the pad, he'd written, "Sophie." It had taken the better part of three days, snatching whatever time he could in the office between meetings, to come up with a plan to persuade Sophie to give this lawyer a chance.

Before he lost his nerve, and the afternoon work demands overwhelmed him, he clipped on his headphones and dialed the eight one eight number Sophie had so reluctantly given him.

"Sophie Reid," she answered crisply.

Ryan paused, flustered. She sounded so grown up and well dressed on the phone. He'd been imagining her far more vulnerable and, well, naked.

"Can I help you?" Her voice broke the static filled air.

Thank goodness he was wearing headphones otherwise he probably would have dropped an ordinary receiver into the cradle out of sheer embarrassment.

"It's Ryan. Ryan Becker," he echoed her no-nonsense tone. Wow. That was stupid. She already knew his name.

A quiet "Oh" was all he heard through his headset.

Unsettled by the sparseness of her side of the conversation, he waded in. "First, I'm sorry I didn't call before now. I've been swamped at work. But I've devised an eleven-point plan to get you to orgasm," he said, dropping to a whisper with the last word.

Sophie laughed. The full throaty sound arrowed straight to his groin. "Not a ten or twelve point plan?"

"No, eleven is the number I ended up with." He cleared his throat. "Anyway, the plan is predicated on you coming out with me Friday night."

"I think maybe that's something I can agree to." She hesitated. "What's the catch, Mr. Three Syllable Man?"

Did he sound that much like a pompous lawyer? He was going to have to get more friends who spoke plain English. "The only catch is that our date, so to speak, would be in Big Bear. And it wouldn't be just Friday, but the weekend as well."

"What time are you picking me up?" she asked.

Wow. That was much easier than he thought it would be. He'd expected her to grill him on his eleven-point plan. He'd made a dozen bullet points to convince her to go. She never ceased to surprise him.

"T-two o'clock okay?" he stammered. "I, um, looked up the production schedule for your show and it seems that you're off…"

"Yep. Studio teacher said the kids' hours were too low. Nothing you can do about that. I'll see you Friday."

"Oh, you can bring Sasha," he said before she could hang up.

"Cool." She rang off.

He pressed the disconnect button on his wireless head-phones and yanked them off, dropping them unceremoniously on his desk. Standing before his view of the ocean, he raked a hand through his hair and shook his arms, trying to rid himself of the nervous feeling that had gripped him during the entire call.

Looking at the tent in his pleated pants, he wondered how he could ever have thought she wasn't his type. Everything about Sophie made him hot, from the sexy rasp in her voice to the slight protrusion of her dusky areolas. His mouth watered at the prospect of feeling her hard nipples in his mouth again. He swore there and then, he would do things right this time, delaying his own pleasure for as long as he needed. He leaned his forehead against the cool glass, placing his outstretched hands above him.

The sound of a light knock and his heavy wood door opening shook him from his reverie. "Ryan, do you need anything before I cut out for lunch?"

Thank goodness he had the presence of mind not to turn around when Evangeline poked her head in. The last thing he needed was a sexual harassment claim. "Can you call the realtor and confirm the Big Bear reservations when you get back? I'll e-mail you some files I need after your lunch break," he called over his shoulder.

"Will do, boss," Evangeline said, mock saluting him before closing the door behind her.

Ryan reviewed a few agreements with various actors, writers, and directors before he quit for the day. The impending weekend weighed heavily on his mind. His promise to be the first lover who would bring her to fulfillment, so to speak, was a huge responsibility. It was like deflowering a virgin. He needed help. He couldn't imagine calling his brother or asking his mom for advice, so he high-tailed it out of his fourteenth story office and headed over to the biggest bookstore within driving distance.

He generally wasn't a fan of the huge mega bookstores with their in-house coffee bars, but he was professionally trained to turn to books when he needed an answer to a particularly difficult issue, and shaking that kind of habit was not easy. He prowled around the bookstore, having no idea where to begin to look. He rebuffed help from a twenty-something employee, too embarrassed to explain his needs.

Finally, he came upon a "Sex, Love, & Relationship" section in the far corner of the third floor. Ryan browsed titles that promised to school him in the art of seduction or make him dummy proof when it came to sex. He flipped through a couple of books and made his choices, not quite meeting the eyes of the checkout girl as he handed over his platinum credit card.

He stayed up far too late reading, and taking notes on his trusty yellow pad. He was going to be ready for the weekend.

SEVEN

SOPHIE'S BEDROOM looked like a tsunami had hit. In her haste and nervousness, she had strewn clothes everywhere. What did one pack for a weekend that was going to be filled with either sex—in which case she'd be naked most of the time—or, if he gave up on his eleven-point plan, a number of long walks through the woods with the dog in tow? She wanted to believe that she would finally experience the kind of sexual release that books and songs were written about and wars were fought over, but deep down it felt hopeless.

She ran to the den and checked the Big Bear temperatures on her laptop. It was definitely sweater weather out there—a full twenty degrees cooler than the Valley. She haphazardly threw together a couple of pairs of jeans and a few of her less outrageous sweaters, and pulled her shearling lined leather jacket from the back of the closet. She yanked on a black turtleneck and jeans, and pushed her hair, still dyed Goth black from yesterday, into a checkered newsboy cap and set it at a jaunty angle.

Sasha followed her to the kitchen as she bagged kibble, a couple of chews, and plastic bowls for the dog.

She nearly jumped out of her skin when Sasha started barking before the doorbell chimed. It took a few deep breaths before she could work up the nerve to open her front door. Her mouth almost went dry at the sight Ryan. How had she forgotten how hot he was?

The white turtleneck he wore highlighted his broad shoulders, flat stomach, and lightly tanned skin. She balled her hands at her sides, though she was itching to run her fingers through his hair, and trace his slightly stubbly jaw line. His hair was getting a little long in the back, and curled deliciously along his collar.

The dog was not nearly as inhibited as Sophie was. She had no problem showing her excitement. She launched herself off Ryan's legs, encased in fawn corduroys, and spun in happy little circles. He dropped to his haunches to pet the dog, letting Sasha lick his face enthusiastically.

He stood again, his six-foot three frame towering over her. "Sasha's obviously ready to go. You packed?"

Sophie nodded, not trusting her voice. She turned around to haul her bag to the car, but Ryan took the bags from her. "I've got that." He nestled her hot pink duffel and floral tote bags in the trunk alongside his sturdy and very masculine-looking black leather weekender. "Do you need anything for the dog?"

She found her voice. "Everything is in the tote. I'll just get her leash." She turned back to the house and then looked back at him leaning against the car, arms and legs crossed oh-so-casually. "Are you sure that it's okay to put Sasha in your car?"

"It's just fine," he insisted.

She got Sasha's lead off the peg by the door. The jangle of the leash excited the dog so much that it took a couple of minutes for Sophie to actually hook the leash on the dog's collar. She was going to have to look into dog training when she came back. She locked the door behind her, set the alarm, and took a deep breath. As soon as she got into his car, she knew she was committed to whatever the weekend might bring.

The early afternoon traffic flowed surprisingly smoothly and Sasha quickly settled down on the quilt covering the back seat. When they hit the Foothill freeway, Sophie relaxed a little, settling into uneasy silence for the long hour and a half ride ahead.

After a time, using the steering wheel controls, Ryan quieted the jazz that always seemed to play in his car like background music. "You okay? You're a bit quiet over there," he said, glancing at her for only a moment.

"Holly's pregnant," Sophie blurted out, then covered her mouth, instantly regretting the outburst.

Ryan mouthed, *Wow*, his eyes trained on the road.

"I shouldn't have said anything," Sophie backtracked. "Promise you won't mention it," she pleaded.

"I'm the soul of discretion," he promised. "What is she going to do?"

"Have the baby. She's wanted a family for a really long time. It's the man part she's having a hard time fitting into the equation."

"How does Nick feel? He is the father, right? They seemed pretty cozy at Korby."

"He doesn't know," she said. Realizing how bad it sounded, she tried to amend the statement. "It's a long story. She has her reasons. Damn, I've said too much already."

"I guess she has a lot to think about," Ryan said evenly. Not taking his eyes off the road, he showed her how the car's stereo system controls worked. "Why don't you pick something you'd like to listen to?"

She settled on Power 106. Hip hop blared through the speakers before she turned the volume down a micrometer. "Sorry," she shouted.

He quirked an eyebrow.

"You get used to it," she explained. "I spend every day with teenagers."

RYAN STOLE a glance at the woman next to him. Christ almighty. What in the hell was he thinking that he could go even a couple of hours without touching her? It was a good thing he drove a stick shift. He *had* to keep both hands free to operate the car. That voice, those lips. With every breath she took, every bump of the car made her small breasts bounce. Did she ever wear a bra? If it were legal, and they didn't have an innocent dog with them, he would have pulled across all six lanes of traffic and initiated her in the ways of backseat sex.

He glanced at the dashboard navigation system. Forty miles to go. Mentally reviewing the information he'd gathered from his nighttime reading, he was relieved that he had decided to try something several of the books mentioned. The minute they arrived he would get a handle on things, so to speak, to delay his pleasure, and enhance hers. It had never occurred to him to seek his own release before he met a woman for a date. The heightened anticipation and tension had always been a part of the fun. But that anticipation had spelled disaster for him and Sophie last time. This time he wanted to be fully in control.

Imperceptibly, he shifted in his seat, glancing down briefly. It wasn't a full salute, but there was a slight chafing against the fly of his pants. He kept his eyes forward and tried to think of neutral topics he could ask her about. Ryan turned the music down to a manageable level and she looked over at him expectantly.

"Do you have any other brothers or sisters?" he asked, sounding lame to his own ears. It was such a stupid first date kind of question.

"It's just me and Selie," she responded.

"What's she like?"

"She's the Marcia Brady of my life," she said, laughing awkwardly. "She's gorgeous, and everything in her life goes pretty much perfectly. She went to the right schools, married the right guy. My niece is positively angelic. Somehow my dear sister manages to 'have it all.' You'd love her. Everyone does."

He let her wind down before he spoke again. "If I ask you something, will you finally give me a straight answer?"

She sighed and pouted like a thirteen-year-old. Her taste in music wasn't the only thing she had picked up from her teenage charges. She slouched in her seat, prop ping her perfectly painted purple toenails on the dashboard, and blew air at the few wisps of hair that had escaped the front of her hat. "Just ask me, Ryan."

"It's the lawyer thing. Is it all lawyers, or just me?"

Two miles were added to the odometer before she answered. Her husky voice was muted.

"My father, you know, the guy who disappeared Daisy —he was—*is* a lawyer," Sophie said, apparently trying for a nonchalance she did not quite achieve. "It's just that I grew up with someone dictating how my life was going to be. I promised myself when I moved out on my own that I would never be in a relationship where a guy tried to run my life."

"But why write off a whole profession? Doctors or, I don't know, accountants, or *anyone* could treat you like that."

"You're one hundred percent right. It's just that it's an easy solution. Most people, thank goodness, are not lawyers, so it's a bright line rule that works for me," she said, turning around to check on the still sleeping dog.

"I would never treat someone I'm dating like that."

She sat up straight as they left the Foothill freeway and turned onto the beautifully scenic City Creek Road. The two-lane highway wound up into the mountains and the noise and chaos of the freeway and the city sprawl fell away behind them. Pine studded hills rose and fell as they made their way toward Big Bear Lake.

Sensing the change, Sasha woke up. Ryan opened a rear window and the dog impatiently pushed her wet nose through the crack.

"Well, we're not really dating, are we?" He barely

heard Sophie's delayed reply over the hum of the radio and air blowing through the window, but he got her message loud and clear, and something pulled uncomfortably tight in his gut. It irked him that he never knew where he stood with her. *He* certainly thought their relationship constituted dating. Maybe they hadn't gone about it in the traditional way, but he had a plan to fix that—starting in less than an hour. Would there be anything between them after this weekend? He really hoped so, but he'd let her make that decision for herself, after—well, after he had time to convince her, of course. He was a lawyer and persuasion came naturally.

IT WAS BIG. Huge, really. That was Sophie's first thought when Ryan steered the car into a wide stone driveway. The house was large and rambling and beautiful. Like a number of houses she'd seen scattered along roads called Woodside and Stoney Creek and Echo Hill, this one was built from huge logs. Large river rocks adorned the welcoming front stairs.

"This is something else," she said, slightly awed. She didn't know what she had expected, but it certainly wasn't this. Ryan had done good.

He turned off the car and got out, stretching his long legs. "It's on about a third of an acre with a fenced in area for the dog," he said, sounding like a realtor.

"Is it yours?" she asked rather unartfully. Her mother would be horrified at such a rude question.

"No." He laughed, opening the trunk. He pulled out

their bags, unharnessed Sasha, and handed the leash to Sophie. "Lawyering doesn't pay that well."

He dropped the house keys into her hand. She walked ahead and opened the front door. The inside did not disappoint. Sophie loved her small and funky artist retreat in Studio City, but she could get used to something as cozy as this. The interior was a marriage of tongue and groove ceilings and exposed beams. Melon-sized, smooth, blue-gray-green river stones covered the fireplace in the main room from floor to ceiling. She quickly located a back door and let Sasha out, then explored the rest of the house.

The open-plan family, dining, and kitchen areas made up the bulk of the house. Up a short flight of stairs, there were two bedrooms and a couple of bathrooms. Everything was natural—wood, leather, or stone. She couldn't help laughing out loud when she spied the dining and living room fixtures. They looked like deer antlers and were over the top.

Ryan came in carrying various bags. "What's so funny?"

She pointed toward the dining area ceiling.

"I didn't decorate it." He shrugged, throwing up his hands in mock surrender.

Sasha started barking and they went outside to see what she was up to. She'd flushed all sorts of animals from their hiding places in the yard, and the pines swayed with the weight of their small bodies clinging for dear life. Sophie unceremoniously plopped butt on the porch and took in the scene around her. The views were breathtaking. She could see nothing but trees and hills for miles.

Looking down, she could even see the low afternoon sun glinting off the smooth glass sheen of the lake peeking between the trees.

Spontaneously, she grabbed the warm hand Ryan had dropped on her shoulder. "I just want to say thanks for bringing me here. If I forget to tell you later, this is a really nice thing you did." He caught her hand in a firm grip and pulled her up to stand next to him.

The kiss that came was unexpected. It wasn't a fire-stoking kiss like the previous ones that had started conflagrations. It was far more tender and sweet, laced with something more than lust, and it scared the hell out of her.

RYAN WANTED everything to be perfect. So far, so good. He called the dog and she ran in happily. Sophie broke away from their embrace to fill a bowl with water. The grateful dog lapped noisily, her nametag jingling and clinking against the bowl's rim. Sophie leaned against the counter that separated the kitchen area from the dining room table, looking at him expectantly.

"If you're the man with the plan, you had better get cracking."

"Are you hungry?" he asked. When she shook her head negatively, he continued. "Well, later when you do get hungry, we can eat in. I could make something for dinner. Or we could go out. Either way, we should probably stock up on a few groceries." He hoped he didn't sound as nervous as he felt.

They decided to take the dog and picked up some food and wine at a couple of the markets on Big Bear Boulevard. Back in the cabin, Sophie sat behind the counter while Ryan put everything away in the cabinets and fridge.

Self-satisfied, he turned back to her and leaned against the counter. "Your choice." He shrugged, trying for a nonchalant air. "Dinner out or in?"

"Tell me what's on your menu, then I'll decide."

Me, he almost said, and then thought better of it. "Pasta, or—" He sorted through menus the real estate agent had thoughtfully left on the counter. "Chinese, Japanese, American, French bistro. Apparently, the whole gamut."

She took a long time to consider her options.

"You," she said, pointing in his direction.

His eyes widened; he must have misheard. *You*, in that husky voice of hers, almost gave him a stroke, it had heightened his blood pressure that quickly. He hadn't voiced his thoughts aloud, had he?

"I'll have whatever you're making," she clarified when he didn't respond. It was going to take everything in his arsenal to make it through an entire meal without jumping her bones. So much for the considerate lover.

"If it's okay with you," she said, standing and stretching lazily, "I'm going to shower."

Okay with him? He would be her washcloth if she asked. When he imagined where that small scrap of towel would touch, he almost cut himself with a knife. Sharp cutlery and lustful thoughts did not go together. He focused, and prepped the ingredients for dinner. When she didn't come back after a few minutes, he lit kindling in the fireplace, and dimmed the lights everywhere except the kitchen.

Ryan padded in his stocking feet to the nearest guest bathroom and looked at himself in the harsh light. Turning away from the mirror, he unzipped his pants and released his semi-erect penis from his boxer shorts. This had better work. The last thing he wanted was to come up soft when Sophie was ready to consummate their union. The book had promised that relieving himself early would make it easier to focus on Sophie's pleasure without rushing things to satisfy his own. It only took a few moments for Ryan to be fully hard.

He envisioned Sophie's full lips; the small breasts unfettered, and imagined her throaty voice whispering in his ear, hoarse with satisfaction. His hand slicked with lotion, he was quick to bring himself to gratification. While cleaning himself up, Ryan looked at his reflection. Now that he'd worked off the edge of anticipation, he had to admit that he certainly appeared and felt a lot calmer.

Sophie still hadn't returned, so he gave Sasha some kibble and let her out to do her business. When he came in from the backyard, Sophie was sitting at the counter, her back to him, as cool as a cucumber, sipping at a glass of wine. It was only when he got closer, and she turned around to face him, did he realize what she had done.

EIGHT

RYAN'S HAND shot out of its own volition and he touched her hair. It was all natural, and it was beautiful. The flickering firelight danced off her reddish gold hair, which hung just past her chin in delicate waves. That was not the only change. She was no longer covered from top to bottom in black. Instead of the turtleneck and jeans from earlier, she was perched on the stool dressed only in a gray silk kimono. Her slim legs and perfectly formed feet draped over the edge of the stool. The red and gold of the dragon elaborately embroidered on the robe complimented her hair perfectly. He suddenly lost his appetite… for food.

He got down on one knee before her, the symbolism of the gesture lost on neither one of them, and took her small hand in his. "Can you promise me something?"

She hesitated a long moment, apprehension apparent in her soft gray eyes. "Sure. What?"

God, he was scaring her when he meant to do just the

opposite. He changed his approach. "Have you ever done yoga?"

She nodded, obviously perplexed now. "I've gone with Holly a couple of times…Why?"

He shook his head. This wasn't working. He was having a hard time finding the right words to prepare her for what was to come. "Are you hungry?"

She looked even more confused. "I'm not following you. Do you want me to promise to go to yoga with you? This weekend?"

He shook his head again. Actions were better than words. "Come here," he said, his voice already roughened by desire. He grabbed her hand and they made their way over to the faux bearskin rug before the hearth. The now roaring fire dispelled some of the chill in the cool night air. In spite of the warmth, she stood, arms and legs crossed awkwardly as if she were freezing to death. He got their wine glasses and shut off the kitchen light. There was no moon and the room was thrown into near darkness. The only illumination of the room came from the flickering fire and the stars twinkling through the uncovered floor to ceiling windows.

"I can't cook or think about eating right now."

"Oh," she said and sat down gracefully, crossing her legs, and arranging her kimono primly across her lap.

"Are you wearing anything under that robe?"

SOPHIE LOOKED into Ryan's eyes and shook her head oh-so-slowly. "No."

He sat down facing her, his long legs stretched before

him. They were hip to hip. She grabbed her wineglass from the hearth, ready to take a big gulp. At this point, she needed all the alcohol-induced courage she could muster. He looked as if he wanted to eat her up in a single bite.

"No more," he insisted. Ryan grabbed her hand before she could raise the wine to her lips again. "I want you as sober as a judge tonight."

During the very long rinse in the shower, it had seemed like a good idea to get rid of the Goth black hair. If Ryan really wanted her, or even if he was going to reject her, she wanted his decision to be based on the *real* her. Now, she was second guessing that decision. Despite the cool silk robe covering her fire-warmed body, she felt naked before him. Without the artifice of carefully applied makeup or temporary hair dye, or even the bravado of intoxication, she had run out of barriers to erect between Ryan and herself.

She set her untouched wine down, and he lifted her effortlessly onto his lap. Instinctively, she straddled his hips with her thighs and looped her arms around his neck for support.

"Ryan, I'm too heavy," she said self-consciously. "I don't think—"

He brought a single finger to her lips. "Don't think. Just feel."

When his lips met hers, she closed her eyes and tried to do exactly what he said. It did feel good, really good. Her body thrummed with nervousness and excitement and, slowly, arousal. He didn't push her or do anything that made her uncomfortable. All he did was kiss her like he couldn't get enough of her. He brushed his lips against her forehead, anointed her closed eyes, each cheek, the freckles on the bridge of her nose, and again settled on her mouth. He kissed her from every angle imaginable, but nothing more. And by degrees, Sophie relaxed.

She opened for him when his tongue tentatively skated across the seam of her lips. She was ready for more. He tasted like wine and desire. Her skin pulled taught with arousal. She started to feel like she had an itch she couldn't scratch. She was seated in the most intimate way imaginable, but she wanted, somehow, to be closer to him. Unconsciously, she ground her hips against the hard ridge of his erection trapped in his corduroys, but it wasn't enough. He pulled his mouth from hers, and Sophie looked down at the instrument of so much pleasure. God, it was a sexy mouth. A man should not be allowed to walk the earth with a mouth that sensuous.

Heavy lidded, he looked her in the eyes again, and slowly unknotted the belt of her silken robe. He looked down at her nude body as he pulled the robe apart. He stared at her for a long, seemingly interminable moment.

She squirmed under his silent scrutiny. "What are you looking at?"

"You. I'm looking at you," he whispered, his voice filled with reverence. "You're so very beautiful." When she shook her head disbelievingly, he tipped her chin up, blue eyes meeting gray.

"Trust me on this," he said pressing her hand over his erection. She could feel how hard he was even through layers of cotton and corduroy. "You have the most lovely eyes. The sexiest lips I've ever tasted. Everything about you is perfect for me."

He traced the delicate column of her throat with a single finger and smoothed his large hands along her collarbone. Openmouthed, he kissed her. It was searing, hot, and passionate. Their breathing quickened. The only sounds in the room were the crackling fire and their mingled breaths. Her pulse sped up, beating in time with the sudden heavy throbbing of her sex. The urge to squeeze her thighs together and relieve the building pressure was thwarted by the large man between them. She pulled back, breathless. "Ryan, I want, oh God, I don't know, more," she panted. "This is killing me."

He silently followed her cue, dragging a throw pillow from the leather couch, and gently easing her down on the rug. The silk robe fanned out on both sides of her slim body, laying her bare before him. Her need for fulfillment and her desire to pleasure him outweighed the urge to cover what she could with her arms. He lay next to her, propped on one elbow, gazing down at her. The other free hand he smoothed down her torso, stopping to whisper against her beaded nipples, sweeping lightly across her concave belly, only dusting the curls that hid her sex from his view.

She shivered in the warm heat. He lightly pinched one hard nipple between his fingers, while he swooped down and pulled the other deeply into his warm mouth. The combination of sensations took her by surprise and her hips bucked of their own accord. Every touch from Ryan felt divine, but she still felt incomplete somehow. She slid her hand down, and parted her nether lips seeking her own clitoris. Ryan, sensing her movement, stopped his ministrations.

"Let me," he said, easing her hand away slowly. He kissed his way down her stomach, tickling her navel with his tongue. He kissed her inner thighs and she held her breath in silent anticipation. Positioning her legs on his shoulders, he kissed her core as passionately as he had made love to her mouth. His hands snaked up, each gently squeezing a breast, then took both nipples between his fingers, squeezing gently. The myriad sensations coalesced, and almost sent Sophie over the edge. Almost. She couldn't quite make it to the finish line. Her toes curled in anticipation, and her breath caught in her chest, then nothing.

Ryan pulled his mouth away, inching up until he was lying next to her. "Sophie, hon, can you try something for me?"

Sophie nodded, not looking at him, trying not to cry. She let out her breath in a muted hiss, her arousal dying slowly, by degrees. She had wanted so much for this to work.

SHE LOOKED BEAUTIFUL; her breasts gleamed as if anointed by the firelight. Sophie was truly an enigma. He was having trouble reconciling her evocative manner with her conservative panties and her obvious inexperience. He gathered what was left of his wits. "I wouldn't normally ask this question, but have you had this issue with other lovers?"

Sophie squeezed her eyes shut, and threw her slim arm across her face, like a child playing hide-and-go-seek in plain view. "There aren't a score of other 'lovers,' Ryan, just a couple of boyfriends."

"By a couple, you mean just two?"

"Just two, Ryan. Evidently, I'm not a desirable woman."

He ignored the last part of her statement. The bulge in his pants said otherwise. At her age, he'd expected her to have more experience. Though he would never admit it, he was thrilled that she'd chosen him. He decided to probe further because he needed all the knowledge he could get to muster an assault on her defenses.

"And they weren't able to bring you to, uh, fulfillment?" he asked tentatively.

She shook her head. "My first was my high school boyfriend," she started, her voice unusually timid. "We dated most of my junior year, but we were just high school kids, you know? And my expectations were pretty low. So I wasn't disappointed that the earth didn't move or anything. My last boyfriend, Andy, was…is an actor who's more interested in recreational drugs than in sex. When he was high, he was always horny. That's when I started drinking a lot of wine to try to…catch up to him."

Ryan swore under his breath, his right hand fisting as he thought of smashing this pretty boy actor in the face. He relaxed his hand and grasped Sophie's in his, removing her arm from her face.

It killed him that other men hadn't loved her with the skill and care she so obviously needed and deserved. Sure, some women enjoyed a quick roll in the hay. But his experience was that most women needed time and patience. A lot of sensuous foreplay was just fine with him. He felt compelled to eliminate any doubts she may have about his desire for her.

Unceremoniously, he pulled off his shirt, pants, and underwear, until he was as naked as she.

Without fanfare, he swallowed her small hand in his and brought their hands to his throbbing penis. Sophie snatched her hand away as if she had come to close to a burning flame.

She opened one eye and snuck a look at him. "You're turned on?" she asked incredulously.

"Of course," he answered matter-of-factly.

Both eyes were open now, and staring directly at his fully erect penis, which twitched toward her, of its own volition. "By me?"

"God, yes," he hissed.

He lay flat and she sat up, leaning over him. It was a beautiful sight. Her hair shone golden in the firelight. Her dusky tipped breasts bobbed achingly close to his lips. He pulled her hand back to his body, this time settling their hands over his rapidly beating heart. She didn't pull away this time. Her gaze was questioning, though her lips remained silent.

"I'm nervous too, Sophie," he admitted. He brought her hand to his lips, kissing the pads of her fingers one by one. "I want you to feel the same pleasure that I feel whenever I look at you, or touch you, or kiss you. Do you remember earlier when I asked you to do something for me?"

She nodded, enraptured.

"I want you to relax. You're like an athlete tense with performance anxiety. Whenever you feel worked up, like you're on the verge, I want you to breathe like we're taught at yoga. It will make things better for you, I swear."

A TINY FISSURE opened in the armor Sophie wore around her heart, hearing his words. She hadn't known when she got in the car with him that morning that he would be this compassionate. She figured they were both there to enjoy a pleasurable weekend. Here he was, a hot guy—okay, really hot—who could help her reach...well... completion. She always knew he'd certainly reach pleasure in the process. Men always did.

The fact that he cared about her desire, her pleasure, was a pleasant surprise. It was as if something broke free in her chest at her realization. She moved her hand to his broad shoulder and leaned down, closing the gap between them, and kissed him with all of the pent up desire and emotions she had unconsciously held back. Snaking her free hand down, she cupped his balls. She jerked her hand away when he flinched.

She snatched her hand back, gazing at him full of guilt. "I'm sorry, did that hurt?"

"Hurt? No," he said shaking his head ruefully. "Hell, Sophie, you could never hurt me. It just felt damned good. Really, really good. That's all."

"Can I touch you again?" she asked, eager now. "Show me how to please you."

"You don't have to do anything else to make me feel good. Just looking at you makes me rock hard."

· · ·

SHE KISSED HIM AGAIN, her tongue dueling earnestly with his, her sneaky little hands tweaking his flat nipple one minute and lightly stroking his cock from base to tip the next minute. Ryan pointedly slowed his breathing, very glad he'd relieved a little of this pressure earlier. With the little siren touching him like this, holding back his pleasure was teeth-grittingly difficult. But he could do it.

Something in the way he and Sophie were touching and relating had changed. He grasped the ripe peach of her buttocks, slid her up his body and pulled one hard nipple into his mouth. Ryan was rewarded when an unexpected moan escaped from Sophie's lips. Her knees were straddling his hips now, as she braced herself on his shoulders and ground herself against his erection. Her breath came in gasps and husky little moans now. She was so close. A little push and she'd be over that cliff.

He cupped one breast in his palm, using his thumb to delicately stroke the hard nubbin at the center. He slid the other hand between them and gently stroked her clitoris, slick with her arousal. Her moans stopped as she held her breath in anticipation.

"Breathe," he whispered fiercely.

A few deep breaths later, Sophie came with a keening cry. He had a screamer on his hands. If Ryan hadn't been aroused to the point of pain, he would have pumped his fist in the air and whooped with satisfaction. He felt that triumphant.

Before Sophie's ardor cooled, Ryan changed their positions so that she was beneath him. He quickly sheathed himself and at her nod, entered her. He almost came apart when he felt her inner muscles squeeze him, still quaking with the aftershocks of her orgasm. With her lips swollen from their kisses and her hair askew, she looked so thoroughly satisfied, and he felt himself grow even harder.

Ryan kept his strokes slow, rekindling the fire of her desire. He kissed her again until her eyes glazed over, and stroked each nipple until she tossed her head from side to side. Reaching between them again, he stroked her hard, desire-slick clitoris until she screamed a second time, and only then did he allow himself to pump furiously, roaring as his own orgasm pulsed through him.

He withdrew from her achingly slowly, both of them reluctant to break their bond, and took care cleaning up. When he came back, she was laying on the rug nude, robe abandoned, with a smug, self-satisfied smile.

"That was great. Can we do it again?" Sophie asked cheekily.

"Oh, honey, I'm not eighteen anymore," he said, making himself comfortable in front of the fire.

He grabbed her hand, intertwining their fingers. His hands swallowed hers, but it didn't stop him from noticing that one of her perfectly manicured fingernails was chipped. It was an endearing imperfection. The sex between them had been good, especially for her this time. But this, lying here quietly just holding her hand, was pretty special too. The feeling of warmth and contentment arrowed straight to his groin.

Sophie didn't miss a thing. She looked at his cock, which was coming back to life in spite of his words. "I think your body disagrees."

. . .

SOPHIE WOKE up to the smell of bacon. For a few disori-
ented moments she didn't remember falling asleep or
where she was. The crackling fire and half-naked man in
the kitchen swiftly brought her back to reality. Clad only
in well-fitting boxers and an apron, Ryan was clanging
pots and pans, ostensibly preparing a late night meal for
them. After she scouted her kimono, she pulled on the silk
robe and belted it tightly. She grabbed the wineglasses
and made her way to the kitchen counter. She sat and
watched Ryan's lithe movements as he moved through the
kitchen, seemingly at home. The dog sat on the braided
kitchen rug, ears erect, watching Ryan's every movement.

"What's for dinner?" Sophie asked.

"Spaghetti carbonara," he said, working quickly to add
pasta, eggs, and cheese to bacon he had sautéed, and
before she knew it, plates of steaming food appeared on
the counter. Ryan handed her a napkin and utensils,
before doffing the apron. He leaned toward her, and she
pulled back reflexively, looking down at the smooth front
of her silk kimono.

"Did I drop something?" she asked, her eyes roaming
her lap.

Ryan colored. "I was going to kiss you. That's all."

Sophie sat mute. "Oh," was all she finally said, feeling
uneasy with him again. They were sitting here like civi-
lized people when they'd just done the naked mambo
hours before. He'd seen her exposed. He'd heard her
come. She wanted him to kiss her, but she also wished to
disappear into the floor. Would these feelings ever go
away?

He came around and sat next to her. Awkwardness

aside, Sophie didn't realize how hungry she'd become. Rather than look at Ryan, and risk him seeing her embarrassment, she dug into the meal with gusto.

"This is good," she complimented. "What else do you make?"

Ryan shrugged. "Mostly pasta dishes. My mother didn't cook much and my brother and I taught ourselves to make quick, filling meals."

Sophie looked at him as if seeing him for the first time. They were getting into the forbidden "relationship" territory. Part of her wanted to know more about his family, but it invited intimacies she didn't necessarily want to return. Unfortunately, her brain didn't have quick enough control over her mouth and she blurted out her question before she could censor her thoughts.

"Did your mom volunteer a lot or work at a job or something?"

Ryan's eyes grew flat. "My mom cleaned other people's houses."

Trying to overcome the uneasiness she felt, Sophie immediately filled the silence with another question. "What about your dad?"

He took his empty plate from the counter and made a noisy production of loading the dishwasher and scrubbing pots and pans. "My dad worked on the line at The Brewery until he was killed in an accident there." Sophie barely heard him above the clang of the water hitting metal. His face was turned away. She could only guess at what he was feeling.

"I'm sorry," Sophie said so softly she wasn't sure he heard. His family was as different from hers as night was from day. Her family had always had one housekeeper or another who came twice a week to "do the heavy work" as her mother called it. She'd never cleaned a toilet or mopped a floor until she was in her twenties, out on her own.

When the water shut off, Ryan spoke. "It's not the answer you expected, was it?"

"It's rare that parents of people our age have died. I'm sorry to hear it," she said, dodging the other issue. She knew that she'd grown up with more advantages than most in the affluent Los Angeles suburb of San Marino. She generally avoided the topic since she had left the privileged social circles her parents and sister still circulated in. Her coworkers were generally hourly union workers like herself, but they lived paycheck to paycheck. She knew she'd started out ahead of the game and had some savings to buffer her through hard times and emergencies. Despite the difficult relationship with her parents, she always knew in the back of her mind she could count on them if things ever got really difficult for her.

Sophie picked up her empty plate and joined him at the sink. She didn't want to care about him like this, but something deep within her wanted to reach out and soothe away Ryan's lingering pain of growing up without money or both parents. She lowered her husky voice a full octave. "Why don't we bank the fire and go to bed?" There was no question of them taking up separate bedrooms at this point.

He looked down at her, his eyes at half-mast, full of renewed sensual hunger. "Now that's a good idea."

NINE

SOPHIE WOKE with Ryan's broad muscular back dominating her vision. The bedcovers had slipped to his waist, and she was rewarded with inches of touchable flawless skin. She resisted the urge to trace its well-muscled contours. Her hand firmly at her side, she roamed him with her eyes from the too-long hair, the silky blond curls resting at the strong column of his neck, to the indentation of his spine that arrowed straight to the firm muscular butt, which she could only imagine under the covers. Her stomach dipped when she thought of last night. It had been incredible. She could finally see how fulfilling sex could be addictive. Already she craved more of him to satisfy a growing itch she'd studiously ignored all these years.

She was so deep in thought, she was startled to hear Ryan speak. He'd turned in her direction without her notice.

"Good morning, Sunflower," he said, his voice roughened by sleep. He smiled lazily and hooked a finger on the blanket and sheet pulling the covers down to her waist, so she too was laid bare from the waist up. She felt naked and exposed to his gaze. There had been no thought of foraging for her pajamas among her luggage when they'd finally gone to bed last night. Putting on more clothes had been the last thing on her mind. She tried not to be self-conscious as he gazed at her in the bright morning light, filtered only by gauzy curtains covering the floor to ceiling windows. Neither of them had thought to pull the heavy drapes the night before.

Sophie couldn't figure out where to put her shaky hands before Ryan noticed. He didn't miss a beat, though.

"You nervous?" he asked. When she nodded gravely, he continued. "Why?"

She gestured toward the windows. "It's kind of bright in here."

He glanced at her breasts, causing her nipples to peak. He smiled devilishly. "I like it that way."

Sophie glanced at the bedroom door. "Should we check on the dog, let her out, feed her?"

"Shhh. She'll be fine for a little bit," he said laying a single square-tipped finger across her lips. "It's early yet." He traced that same finger down the side of her neck, across her shoulders, and circled her protruding areola.

"I can't believe you don't know how sexy you are. Every time I see you going commando under one of those skimpy tanks you wear, I can see the outline of your pouty nipples and I want to lift your shirt and take you in my mouth."

She squirmed, feeling her juices flow. She was getting aroused just hearing his words. He hadn't even really touched her yet. The anticipation of more words or more actions was setting her teeth on edge. She waited to see what would come next. His eyes were heavy lidded and knowing. He leaned toward her, circling her areola with his finger again, then darted his quicksilver tongue against her pearled nipple, following the path his finger had blazed. The fine hairs along her arm stood on end. Ryan took her breast almost entirely into his mouth, using his tongue to play against the tip.

Sophie's breathing quickened, and she fisted a hand in his hair, bringing his face up to hers. She kissed him, desire spilling from her every pore. He pushed against her palm, and she answered his silent entreaty, holding his pulsing erection firmly in her small grip. Even after doing it a few times, she was amazed that she could make him this hard this fast. In silent appreciation, she swabbed at the small bead of fluid along the tip and looked him in the eye as she took her thumb into her mouth, taking in the essence of him.

He watched her intently, closing his eyes when her lips surrounded her finger. He was still for such a long moment.

She leaned in to kiss his forehead. "You okay?"

When he opened his blue eyes the color of a summer sky, it took everything she had not to look away. "Yeah, you almost sent me over the edge," he said, fighting to control his breathing. "I've never seen anything so hot."

"Do you want to…" she faltered. "Can we…"

"God, yes." He paused. "If you're ready."

She only had to nod slightly before Ryan surged up, jerking open the bedside table and sheathing himself. He spread her legs wide, opening her to him, and hooked her left leg over his shoulder, their bodies lying perpendicular. From this angle, she was completely exposed to him. She knew he could see everything from her pink nether lips to the bobble of her dusky nipples as she gasped.

"Grab the headboard," he instructed. Sophie obliged, grabbing the metal rails on the wrought iron bed, and he entered her with a rush. It felt incredible to have Ryan take her this way, wonderfully overwhelming. She held on for dear life as he pulled out part way and slammed into her repeatedly. Instinctively she hooked her right leg around his buttocks, trying to pull him deeper. Just when she thought she couldn't stand it anymore, he slicked his thumb across her swollen clit, first hard, then soft, then fast, then slow. She closed her eyes and concentrated on her breathing. The orgasm, when it came, took her by surprise, and literally stole her breath. Just as she was coming down from her peak, Ryan climaxed, and his orgasm brought on an unexpected aftershock and a second one for Sophie. She wasn't sure if she blacked out, but it took a few minutes after Ryan withdrew for her to get her bearings. Damn. The man was better than good. She shook her head when he joined her under the blanket.

"What?" he asked, grinning wolfishly.

"I think..." She paused, feeling a little befuddled. "Damn, I think I could get used to this."

He yawned deeply and pulled her against him, her back to his front. He traced her tattoo along its calligraphic lines. Stretching, then yawning again, he whispered, "What's so bad about that?"

After a quick breakfast of cold cereal, Ryan appeared

to be hopping with energy despite the fact that he eschewed caffeine. Sophie was about to suggest they spend the rest of the day in bed, working off that excess energy, but he had on his jacket before she could open her mouth.

"Let's take Sasha for a hike."

Thoughts of a repeat of this morning's performance were already fading from her mind when she reluctantly pulled on her own jacket and thick socks to ward off the morning chill.

Ryan had Sasha leashed and was ready to go by the time Sophie made it to the front door.

"So, nature guy, where are we going today?" she asked, trying to muster up enthusiasm.

"You'll see," he said cryptically.

She was surprised when he unlocked the car doors and harnessed Sasha in the back seat. Only in L.A. did she equate hiking with driving. Out here in the woods, she thought they'd start the hike right from the house. Just another thing she'd been naïve about.

Sophie got into the Acura without comment. Things had gone much better than she'd ever anticipated, so she was happy to go along for the ride. They drove along Route 18. As they snaked in and out of the trees on the winding road, she caught repeated glimpses of the sparkling lake. They turned on Rim of the World and pulled into a deserted parking lot. Ryan popped the trunk and pulled out a fairly large nylon cooler.

"What's in there?" she asked, wondering when he'd had time to do anything like make a picnic.

"Lunch."

They hiked in companionable silence for the first hour. They'd let Sasha off the lead and she ran forward, disappearing around curves, only to run back, making sure they were still following her. For the first time since they'd met, Sophie wasn't feeling insanely nervous around Ryan. The butterflies in her stomach had settled down for once.

They reached a steep incline and Ryan grabbed her hand, helping her up when her short legs faltered. His grip on her hand was firm and reassuring, and if she was honest with herself, really nice. It felt good when he touched her, both in and out of bed. When the path evened out again, he didn't let go, and she didn't pull away, enjoying the constant contact with any part of his body.

After a while he spoke into the silence. "Tell me more about Sophie."

She pulled her hand away, suddenly defensive. "What do you want to know that you already don't?"

He looked as if he wanted to smooth her ruffled feathers. "I don't know your middle name for instance."

Sophie relaxed. Maybe he didn't want to probe her innermost thoughts and feelings which she didn't share with just anyone. "It's Constance."

"Really. What does that name mean? More wisdom?"

"No, worse," she said, shaking her head. "It's just like it sounds, steadfast, constant, you know, not flaky."

Ryan nodded sagely.

"Yeah, you see why my parents were disappointed. I guess they were bargaining for a very traditional child, and they got flighty, artsy me instead." She threw up her hands in mock surrender. "No lawyer, no doctor, no executive, just a make-up artist."

"Do you have that tattooed anywhere on that sexy little body of yours?" He looked at her as if he wanted to peel her clothes off right there. "Maybe I missed something."

Damn, she was nervous again. He needed nothing more than words to arouse her. "The one on my shoulder is the only one I have."

He came back to the subject at hand, asking more about her life.

"I saw some paintings at your house. Are those yours?"

"Nah, those belong to a few artist friends I know around L.A. I dabble in oils a tiny bit. I never took any formal classes or anything like that. My parents thought it was a waste of time. No one can make a career out of art, my father always said. Whatever." She shook her head dismissively. "Let's talk about something else."

"Where did you go to high school?"

"What is this? Are we tripping down memory lane?"

He didn't respond, just waited expectantly.

She sighed. "Flintridge Prep, class of oh two. What about you, Mr. Reseda?"

"Flintridge as in La Cañada-Flintridge?" he asked, referring to one of the wealthiest communities in Los Angeles County.

"Yeah, yeah. I just went to school there, I didn't live there," Sophie said, deflecting further questions about her upbringing. San Marino, in reality, wasn't all that different than La Cañada-Flintridge. But she hated it when people defined her by her parents' choice of hometown. "You didn't answer *my* question," she persisted.

"What you would guess? Reseda High School."

"How did you like it?" she asked, then immediately regretted the question. "I'm sorry, I didn't mean—"

He intertwined their fingers and kissed the back of her hand, sending shivers down her spine. "It's okay. I'm used to the question. It's just public school, not jail. I turned out fine."

"Yeah. You're all right," Sophie said giving him mock punch on the shoulder. Ryan pulled her close and gave her a kiss she felt down to her purple toenails. He pulled back, looking deep into her gray eyes. She wondered if her eyes reflected the stormy passion in his.

"You're a lot more than all right with me," he said, though Sophie was sure there was more than met the eye in those few words.

When they finally reached the top of the trail, the view was breathtaking. There was an uninterrupted view of San Gorgonio Mountain, jagged granite peaks topped with a dusting of early snow. She could see nothing of the vast lake from this area, which backed onto Big Bear. The quiet solitude and spectacular views more than made up for a chance to see Big Bear Lake from such a high vantage point. They veered off the marked trail, and Ryan spread a blanket in a small clearing surrounded by tall pines. He pulled out a portable nylon bowl and filled it with bottled water for Sasha. She drank greedily, then curled into a ball on the edge of the blanket for a much needed puppy nap.

Sharing a meal with someone had never been so

sensual. Ryan fed Sophie tidbits of dried figs stuffed with goat cheese, sparkling white wine, chicken salad, hunks of homemade bread, and small bits of a French chocolate brownie for dessert. He'd even thought about keeping them hydrated with sparkling mineral water. Though she pestered him, she never got an answer about when he'd made or bought all the delicious food.

When talk about the food petered out, they lapsed into another companionable silence. Sophie couldn't remember feeling so comfortable with another person that conversation wasn't necessary all the time they were together. Without talking, she was more attuned to other things: the funny way Ryan's too-long hair kept falling across his forehead even though he kept pushing it back, the flex of his muscles as he made their picnic area more comfortable, how the blue of the sky mirrored the color of his eyes. When their eyes met, hers slid away, unable to meet his gaze. An indescribable feeling filled her. It was a combination of the feeling she'd had when she'd had her first crush on a guy in eighth grade, that youthful mixture of hope and fear of the unknown, and that itchy feeling she got whenever Ryan kissed or touched her.

"Penny for your thoughts?" he said.

She looked up at him, but had to shield her eyes from the strong sun overhead. She reached behind her and fished in her bag, successfully retrieving her sunglasses.

"What's going on in that head of yours?" He didn't so much seem like he wanted to ask a question, but rather wanted to say something else.

"I'll give you a dime for yours."

He pushed aside their picnic remains and held out his

hand. Reflexively she grasped it and he hauled her into his lap.

"Ryan, what are you—"

He slid her sunglasses to the top of her head, traced the rings laddered along the shell of her ear, and pulled her face toward his. This kiss, unlike last night's, didn't set her on fire. Rather, it was tender and giving, and snuck into her heart, grabbed hold, and wouldn't let go.

She pulled back first and started talking before he could. "Have you ever done it in a national forest?"

"No, and I'm not going to start now," he said without much humor.

Sophie wiggled her butt against his growing erection anyway. She wasn't a student of body language, but she could tell Ryan was aroused. Men were easy that way. Another wiggle and Ryan responded as she hoped he would. He stopped talking and started kissing. She looped her arms around his back, pulling him closer and inhaling his wonderfully masculine scent—part soap, part sweat, and all man.

She slipped her hands under his sweater and shirt and dragged her short nails down the smooth warm skin of his back. His kisses grew hungrier. They tumbled back on the blanket, his large frame covering her from head to toe. He quickly did away with her sweater and pushed her tank up, exposing her small breasts to the slightly chilly air. Her nipples hardened. The anticipation of his touch was almost as heady as his touch itself. Almost. He captured a nipple in his mouth, using his lips and tongue to sweeten her arousal. Her hips bucked when his lightly stubbled cheek brushed against her sensitive breasts as he moved from one to give attention to the other. She sucked in a lungful of air when his hands slid down to warm her belly and slid lower to brush against the elastic waistband of her panties.

Sasha's sudden bark broke the spell they'd woven. Ryan pulled up, leaving her suddenly bereft. His hip abutted hers and he rested a hand on the other side of her hip. She was shielded from the view of anyone who happened by. No one came upon their private retreat. They heard the rustle of hikers on the trail who passed them by. Turning back to her, Ryan brushed a wayward lock of hair away from her face.

"You, Miss Reid," he grumbled, "are a distraction." He eased the ribbed white tank down slowly, hiding her from his hungry gaze.

Instinctively she knew he wanted to talk about a relationship or move on to a serious topic, and she wasn't ready to go there with him. Not that he wouldn't be the perfect guy to do that with, the lawyer thing notwithstanding, but serious, "going somewhere" relationships were not in the cards for her. She was a free spirit from her ringed earlobes and crazy hair to her purple toenails. Great sex, now that she had finally experienced it first hand, was in the cards, however, and there wasn't any reason she could think of that they couldn't enjoy each other for as long as that lasted.

"I really like you, Sophie," he said, tracing the freckles that dotted the bridge of her nose. Feeling vulnerable, she scooted back and sat up. She averted her eyes from Ryan and stroked Sasha's soft head as the dog curled in her lap.

"I wasn't planning to say anything to you before the weekend was out—"

She put a single finger to his lips. "I don't want to do this now."

"I know this isn't what you came here for, but we have an incredible connection, and I for one think we should build on it."

She laughed, a harsh sound among the whispering trees. "Like what, go steady?" she asked deliberately, ignoring the sting of rejection she saw in his eyes. "Ryan, I'm not that kind of girl. You knew that when you met me. You need a Seven Sisters, Junior League kind of woman. I'm exactly the opposite of that."

"Don't sell yourself short, you—"

"I'm not selling myself short. I know exactly who I am, Ryan, and why I'm here. I thought we were on the same page. I came up here because we're *physically* attracted to each other and..." She paused, suddenly embarrassed. "Well, you know why."

Ryan rose to his feet and started gathering the remains of lunch, his movements jerky. Sophie stood, and hooked the dog on the leash, giving her a few scratches behind the ears for good measure. When she turned around, he'd folded the blanket. The clearing looked as if they'd never been there.

He pulled on dark, reflective sunglasses, hiding his expressive eyes. "You ready for the trip back down?" His voice was carefully neutral.

She nodded and he tweaked her nose in a brotherly fashion, then started down the hill, walking at a brisk pace.

Sophie had hated saying no to what he may be offering, but she knew it would be unfair to say yes when she couldn't give anything in return. As she pulled on her sweater, the sun and cool breeze seemed to be mocking her. If she'd gotten what she wanted from him, why did she suddenly feel so alone?

SOPHIE WAS SITTING on a chair by the cold fireplace unlacing her trail shoes when the jarring bleat of an old-fashioned telephone startled her.

Ryan dropped the bags in the doorway and sprinted to the phone.

"Are you expecting a call?" she asked, incredulous.

"I gave the number to Evangeline in case of an emergency."

Evangeline? Emergency? What kind of emergencies could a corporate lawyer have? Sophie's father was a federal judge who presided over last minute search warrant requests and death penalty cases and even he almost never received emergency phone calls. She decided to shower the day's sweat and dust off while giving Ryan privacy for whatever was going on with work.

Dressed in jeans and a t-shirt, Sophie's hair was still damp and her feet bare when she came out to the open living area ten minutes later. Ryan was hunched over his little Blackberry so engrossed he didn't seem to notice her or the dog who was dancing around his feet.

He jumped when she tapped him gently on the shoulder.

"Sorry. I was just going to ask about dinner."

"I have to go back to Los Angeles," he said distractedly. At her look of consternation, he clarified. "Tonight."

Sophie stepped back as if she'd been slapped. "Oh. I get it. No problem. I'll get packed up right now." She turned on her heel ready to sprint to the bedroom and hide her mortification. It hit her where it hurt that he didn't want her. She understood why, sort of, but it didn't make it hurt any less.

But before she could put more than a foot between them, he grabbed her upper arm gently, halting her movements. He put down the smartphone and looked her in the eye. "It's not like that. This has nothing to do with us. It's that just something I had hoped was under control blew up at work."

Skeptically, she lifted her pierced brow. "What's so critical that you need to deal with it on a Saturday night?"

"You of all people should understand that I can't talk about this. Confidentiality and all that."

Their easy camaraderie from that morning seemed like a distant memory. In its place was a fragile bond that was growing more tenuous by the moment.

"You know what? You're right. *I* understand far better than you think," she agreed. "My father certainly tutored me in those lessons." Breaking the light grip on her arm, she turned on her heel and marched dejectedly toward the second bedroom where she'd put her luggage.

They drove back to Los Angeles in near silence, Ryan's very adult sounding jazz filling the car's darkened interior.

When he pulled up to her house, it was barely nine o'clock. She looked at the time, thinking dispiritedly of how she was going to fill the rest of the empty weekend hours. Hot wanton sex was not an option at this point. They were uncomfortably silent when she unharnessed the dog and he brought in her bags. She turned on the lights and kicked off her shoes by the door.

Ryan shifted from foot to foot, jingling his car keys. "I don't want to leave things like this."

Sophie plastered a smile on her face. "Don't worry about it. I understand that you have to work."

He looked bewildered. "I still want to see you. As soon as this crisis is over, we should—"

"Why don't we cross that bridge when we come to it?" She gently pushed him toward the door. "Goodnight, Ryan." The heavy wood door closed, the latch catching with a quiet *snick*. She heard his car start and watched his taillights as they disappeared around the corner.

She walked the dog, unpacked her stuff, and ran to the twenty-four hour market to get fresh milk and eggs. She was proud of herself that she'd been able to hold off that long. When she came back at eleven, she broke down. Loud noisy sobs filled the room. Sasha, distressed by the sounds, leaned against her leg as if trying to console her. It was the first time she had cried in years.

TEN

THE BOARDROOM STRETCHED from one side of the building to the other. The twenty-five people surrounding the table were cast in shadow. Speckles of streetlights barely penetrated the floor to ceiling windows lining three sides of the room. Even with subtle lighting from the hidden sconces, darkness swallowed the room. The gloom matched Ryan's mood. Everyone looked like they would rather be anywhere than here. A few were dressed like him in cargo shorts and hiking boots, others in designer eveningwear. But no one was dressed for a last minute strike negotiation session.

Someone's overworked and harried assistant handed out thirty-page packets that laid out the demands of the studios and directors as well as the demands of Local 706. The only sound in the room was the constant flick of pages as the lawyers and union representatives on the negotiating committee scanned the papers they had been given.

Why did these damned contracts always expire at

midnight on a Saturday or Sunday? Were they written that way to make sure negotiators got to the bargaining table before their weekends were ruined? The timing ploy hadn't worked this time. It was coming down to the wire on this one. He shook his head with regret. Unfortunately, the weekend was irredeemable for him and Sophie. There was nothing he could do to get back the magical world they had created in Big Bear. On top of that, he had ended the day, the whole weekend, badly.

After incredible sex that morning, Ryan had wanted to take her on a romantic picnic and tell her that he was falling in love with her. But he'd butchered that completely, only to have to cut the weekend short for this. He slammed the packet closed in front of him, having barely skimmed its contents. He ignored the startled looks from others around the table. Instead, he raked his hand through already mussed hair and blew out a frustrated breath. This was not his finest hour. Thoughts of Sophie crowded work out of his mind.

Keeping the news of an impending strike from her wasn't required by attorney-client confidentiality. He should have told her why he had to leave early even if it had breached some unwritten ethical rule. When he was honest with himself, he knew he had hidden the truth from her because he didn't want her to worry about where her next job or meal would be coming from. Around the table were representatives of the International Alliance of Theatrical Stage Employees. In the industry, they called themselves Local 706. It was Sophie's union of makeup artists and hairstylists and the top union people were threatening to strike unless the studios and producers came to the table with better residual payments, cheaper health care, and more upfront money over the life of the new contract.

Ryan had not buried his head in the sand like an ostrich. He was more than aware, having grown up on the wrong side of the tracks, that it was very expensive to live in Los Angeles. Without pay raises, the union members wouldn't be able to keep up with inflation, not to mention the escalating home prices. On the other hand, it was his job to get across the studio's point of view. With hundreds of cable channels and dozens of entertainment outlets, the viewership for any particular television show or movie was much smaller than it had been in the past.

Gone were the days when Americans only had three television choices and few movie options. Now shows were lucky to make a slim profit, and there just weren't huge piles of money to divvy among the different unions, actors, directors, writers, and below the line workers like Sophie. Studios and producers had to spend every penny wisely. Extravagant pay increases and fully paid health benefits were a thing of the past.

They were getting nowhere and the meeting broke up at two in the morning, the union vowing to go on strike Monday or Tuesday. Ryan looked at his watch. Too late to call her, but he'd be at her house first thing Sunday morning. No need to give up the rest of the weekend even though they were back in Los Angeles.

RYAN SHOWED up unannounced at nine in the morning, greeting a woman too groggy to toss him out on his ear.

She was a mess, red-gold hair askew, raccoon eyes, and rumpled pajamas, but Ryan saw the most beautiful woman in the world. She had become just a little more beautiful overnight. And here he thought he'd shown up at a decent hour. Sophie had seemed like such a morning person only yesterday when they'd made love in the glow of early dawn light. The memory had him grinning like a fool. He knew right then, with a certainty that made him quake, that this woman had snuck her way into his heart and he wasn't going to let her go.

"I didn't think I'd see you again." Sophie's tone was flat.

To say that Ryan was taken aback would be an understatement. How could she think that he wanted to call it quits after the most romantic half a weekend he'd ever had? "You can't shake me that quickly, Sunflower," he said softly, trying to ease her confusion.

"Did you work out your emergency?" She might as well as used air quotes. Sarcasm, anger, and hurt underlied the question.

Ryan opened his hands in supplication. "I guess I can tell you this much. Local seven-oh-six is on the verge of a strike. At the meeting last night the two sides weren't able to even come close to any kind of deal."

"Why couldn't you tell me that yesterday?" she asked, a little less wary than a few minutes ago. "I haven't turned a deaf ear to everything. I've heard talk about a possible strike. It happens almost every year in this town. One union or another gets down to the wire, there's strike talk, then a deal gets worked out and I go to work the next day. It's no big deal, Ryan."

He felt like a heel. He wanted her trust, and she'd given it time and again over the weekend, but he hadn't given his. He'd wanted to protect her, but she was an adult and deserved to know the truth.

Ryan leaned in for a hug. Not wanting to let go of the sleepy body in his arms, he set her back before he got distracted. "Can I ask you for a big favor?"

"It's kind of early. What's up?" Sophie asked warily. She surely thought him demented, standing there like a grinning fool.

Ryan looked at his watch. His Sunday morning brunch with his mother and brother was at eleven. He certainly had time to go home and go it alone. But after that disastrous brunch weeks ago where he'd had to reveal to his brother that he didn't know Sophie's name, he wanted to take her there. He wanted her to meet his family and know the truth about his blue-collar roots.

He'd already been burned, many years ago, when he had proposed to Jocelyn and she'd accepted. He had thought his future was secure—a high-class wife and the perfect job. He'd been sorely disappointed however when Josie had met his family. She'd looked down her straight patrician nose at his mother's work roughened hands and his brother's beat cop uniform. Josie had acted like she'd smelled something bad, or she would somehow get dirty if she stayed too long in his Reseda home. It had sickened him that he'd almost made a huge mistake. It was unfair, he knew, but he wanted to see if Sophie could pass the test.

"Do you want to go to brunch?" he asked. "I go with some people I know almost every Sunday."

She looked at him a little quizzically. "Sure, I guess." She turned and looked in the house as if making up her mind. Then, as if she'd decided something important, she said, "Why the hell not? I never turn down a free meal." She backed into the living room and he followed her in. She looked down at her rumpled clothes. "But I'll need to get ready."

"It's not for another couple of hours..." he added suggestively.

"Ryan, if I'm going to meet your friends, I'm going to need time to prepare." He didn't correct her misunderstanding.

"Can we shower together?" he asked, making a last ditch effort to get in a quickie before they faced his mother's scrutiny. "It'll be more efficient that way." Sex relaxed him more than a stiff drink ever could.

"The guest shower works perfectly well," she said, pointing away from her bedroom. "Though you look as clean as a whistle anyway." He shrugged. He *had* showered before he came over, but a little water never killed anyone.

She shuffled away, slamming the bedroom door hard. He got the message. He wouldn't bother her for the next couple of hours unless he wanted to take his life into his own hands.

When it became clear she was going to use up every last minute before they departed, he wandered around the house looking at the books on her narrow bookshelf and the various paintings she had hung. None of the oils or signatures were familiar, but the bright colors and chaotic abstract art suited her décor and her personality. Sasha whined at his feet and he went with her to the backyard. While the dog relieved herself and sniffed her way along the edge of the fence, he wandered the grassy area. He cocked his head seeing a door that jutted from an addition to the back of the garage he hadn't noticed on his other visits to the house. He twisted the doorknob. It was unlocked.

He entered a small room, painted a cool periwinkle blue. There was one tiny window overlooking the backyard, but the room was awash with diffused light. Ryan looked up. White sailcloth shades partially covered three large skylights. A few canvases leaned in a colorful array against the walls. The canvas on the easel drew his attention. It was an unfinished oil painting of a woman glancing coyly at the viewer. From the bright red hair flowing down the woman's back, Ryan guessed it might be a self-portrait, though it didn't look so much like Sophie, but reflected a universal woman who could represent anyone or everyone.

When he drew closer, though, he saw that the flaming red hair wasn't in fact hair, but dozens of different faces with different expressions—some sad, some happy, a few melancholy, many gleeful. The naked display of emotion on the faces was so raw that he turned away knowing he had somehow breached the protective shell Sophie worked hard to maintain.

He backed from the room as if a specter dogged his every step. Closing the door gently, he corralled the dog and both went into the house. He pulled the television remote control from the basket and flipped through five hundred satellite channels not seeing the various moving images that flickered on the screen.

Everyone in the industry knew there was a certain artistry to makeup. When one saw Hollywood stars up close, they looked nothing like their beautiful on-screen counterparts. But it was a secondary job in an industry where actors and directors were considered the creative giants. He shook his head, awed by Sophie's talent. She had the soul of an artist. How her family could have ever thought she could squeeze her larger than life gifts into the narrow worlds of law or business, he would never know.

The woman that emerged from the bedroom over an hour later was an eclectic blend of the old Sophie and the new Sophie he'd uncovered this weekend. She was Audrey Hepburn meets the Clash.

Touché.

She was doing a little test of her own.

Today she'd paired hot pink hair with a somewhat conservative outfit, for her. The bright floral halter-top festooned with red, yellow, and blue roses hugged her small breasts in all the right places, without revealing too much. But her cute peach of a butt was squeezed into some very short white shorts. The slim legs that extended from the bottom of her short shorts to the tops of her gold strappy sandals were a major distraction. It took all he had to control his desire to pull her back to the bedroom and skip brunch.

Since his mother could get dry toast anywhere, he and Cameron rotated between about four or five of their favorite restaurants for brunch. This week he'd picked an upscale French restaurant on Ventura and Hazeltine that offered a champagne brunch. Leaving his car with the valet, he escorted Sophie in the door. He spotted his mother with her usual glass of plain tap water, and his brother with a mimosa at a window table. Cameron stood at their approach.

"Mom, Cam, I want you to meet Sophie," he said by way of introduction.

SHE WAS GOING to kill him—literally wrap her hands around his attractive throat and throttle him as soon as she had the chance. *Some people* had turned out to be his mother and brother. Her first thought was that Cameron was the more conservative of the two brothers, if it was possible to be more conservative than Ryan. His blond hair and blue eyes mirrored Ryan's, but where Ryan's too-long hair curled at the ends, Cameron's was a severe buzz cut against his head. Though he looked just a little older, Cameron had a few wrinkles around his knowing eyes. An inch or two shorter than Ryan, he was stockier, built like he did pushups for a living.

Unlike her own mother, their mother Bridget was no shrinking violet. Though she looked like she'd worked hard in her life, her faded blue eyes were kind and radiated intelligence. She didn't wear clothes that advertised her widow status. She dressed very hip for her age in a crisp white oxford, black jeans and sequined flats that sparkled in the chandelier's light.

Sophie pulled her hand from Ryan's and shook their hands firmly, then sat down at the table. She debated between taking him out back and throttling him now or waiting until brunch was over. Involuntarily, she shook her head. No, she'd do it slowly, starting now. Honesty was always the best policy.

"You'll have to excuse me," she started. "Ryan neglected to mention that I would be meeting his family today. He mentioned a get together with some *friends*," she said, emphasizing the last word.

Their mom patted her hand, casting a scathing glance at her son. "Oh, dear. I'm sorry about that. You should know I raised my boys to behave better than that. But I promise, we won't bite."

"Thanks." Sophie put on her most endearing smile. "So, have you guys been here before? What's good, Mrs. Becker?"

His mother opened the menu and looked at Sophie. "Call me Bridget, dear," she said. "I've heard that the best dish is the strawberry and cream stuffed French toast."

"That's good enough for me," Sophie said, snapping her menu shut. The waiter came over with a bottle of champagne and offered a glass to everyone at the table. Ryan's mother accepted a glass and Sophie, eyeing Cameron's drink, asked for a mimosa. Ryan had plain tap water.

When the waiter came back this time, they ordered. Sophie and Bridget had the French toast, Cameron eggs Benedict, and Ryan had a Cobb salad, hold the dressing.

When they were all alone again, Cameron spoke. "I hear that you're a makeup artist. How did you end up doing that?"

So, it was going to be that kind of breakfast. Her father, the consummate interrogator, would have been proud. She was grateful when Ryan pulled her hand in his. It gave her the strength and confidence to face anything. "Back when I thought the entertainment industry was exciting, I dropped my major and switched over to that."

Cameron caught the implication in her words.

"Are you that jaded already? You seem kind of young for that kind of cynicism," he said matter-of-factly.

Sophie paused a moment, carefully weighing her response. "Sometimes I imagine doing something else, that's all." She hoped he didn't ask what else she considered doing. Her painting was something she kept very close to her heart.

"Did you grow up in Los Angeles like these boys?" Bridget asked, cutting Cameron off before he could ask more probing questions.

Sophie nodded. "In the San Gabriel Valley," she said, non-committally.

"Pasadena? I occasionally worked over there."

Sophie didn't beat around the bush for once. Evading questions about her background took more energy than telling the truth, and after the weekend she'd had with Ryan, she didn't have the energy for evasion. "No. San Marino, actually."

Bridget paused, nodding knowingly. "What did your father do?"

"Mom, that's enough," Ryan said. "This is not the Inquisition."

"We're fine," Sophie and Bridget said almost simultaneously. Sophie shot Ryan a look that said, *You got me into this*. She turned back to his mom.

"My dad is Harry Reid. He's a federal judge in Pasadena," she answered.

"You'll fit in here perfectly, then. We're a law and order family now. My Cameron's a police officer for the LAPD, and you already know Ryan's a lawyer."

Sophie and Bridget got along like a house on fire. Once she passed Bridget's test, the conversation flowed more smoothly. Sophie had worked on some of Bridget's favorite shows, and was able to give her lots of harmless behind the scenes gossip that would set her cronies' chins wagging. It was the kind of thing she used to impress out of town visitors, but now she knew it worked for the boyfriend's mother as well. Sophie didn't pause to think about the implication of boyfriend. It spelled commitment, and she wasn't about commitment.

They talked for a good hour or so. The obvious tension finally eased from Ryan's shoulders and he looked like he was able to relax and join the conversation. She didn't know why he was so tense if he'd been the one to bring her to brunch, but maybe it was more important to him than she'd realized at first. Throughout brunch, Ryan stayed connected to her even when he wasn't looking her way or talking to her. He rubbed her back briefly, relieving the tension gathered between her shoulder blades. He held her hand when it lay idle. He smoothed his fingers along her bare leg, ostensibly calming her, but doing more to make her think of what they would do to each other later.

After the room emptied and they'd had a number of refills on water and coffee, Cameron looked at his watch meaningfully. "Mom, I have a late shift today, so we've got to get going if I'm going to get to the station on time."

"That's too bad. I was so much enjoying Sophie." She turned to Sophie, grasping her hands. "You've been such a breath of fresh air. Brunch hasn't been this interesting in a long time." Bridget gathered a surprisingly fashionable white denim jacket around her shoulders. Its rhinestones glittered like diamonds. "You'll have to come over for dinner sometime. I'll make one of Ryan's favorites."

"I'd like that very much," Sophie said with sincerity. She had enjoyed spending time with Ryan's mother. Bridget was as different as could be from her parents' contemporaries—who were constantly one upping each other with more expensive cars, ever bigger houses, and more extravagant vacations.

Ryan was quiet for the short ride back to her house. Sophie skirted the house, walking to the small backyard, and opened the back door to greet the excited puppy. Ryan sat under the patio umbrella, extending his long legs casually, crossing them at the ankle. When she finally sat, he turned to her, his eyes serious.

"Thanks."

"For what? Your mom was great and your brother was nice, though he scares me a little," she admitted.

"Cameron can be a bear sometimes. I think he takes his 'cop' persona too far, but he's fiercely loyal to Mom. He does everything he can to make her more comfortable."

"Is she still working?" Sophie asked hesitantly.

"Nah." He shook his head. "Not that it wasn't a fight getting her to retire. But between Social Security and the two of us, we've got her covered. We can't get her to leave the old neighborhood, though." He curled his fist. "We tried to get her into a new condo years ago, but she's got everything she could want out there, I think."

Sophie patted his arm. His bicep tensed reflexively. "It's good to see a parent-child relationship that works." She looked off into the distance, staring at nothing in particular. She tried not to be jealous when she met people whose parents so obviously cared for them. She knew deep in her heart that her parents loved her. But she would never have the easy camaraderie of Ryan and his mom — the nitpicking and constant criticism got in the way of that.

Ryan grabbed her hand, intertwining their fingers. "Come here," he said gruffly, hauling her onto his lap. "I'm sorry we had to end the weekend early."

"It's okay. You had to work."

"It *was* work, Sophie," he said with finality, dismissing any thoughts of rejection from her head. "It had nothing to do with us."

She put her hands flat on his broad chest, ready to push herself off his muscular thighs. Why did he have to make it all so complicated? She was fine with just hot, mind-blowing sex.

He stilled her movements. "Don't run."

She settled more comfortably in his lap, though her heart beat a mile a minute. Of its own volition, her hand reached around him, stroking the vulnerable area at the nape of his neck. At his deep intake of breath, she started to pull back.

He sensed her hesitancy. "It's okay. I love it when you touch me."

She continued to stroke him, running her hand through the silky curls at his nape. "It's not...I'm not coming on to you...I don't know."

"It's okay to want to touch me. I like the way you feel." He weaved their fingers, her small pale hand in stark contrast to his larger, tanned one. "I like holding your hand, knowing that you're close by my side." He laid their joined hands near his heart. She could feel each beat pulse beneath their fingers. Tentatively, she laid her head on his shoulder. She felt overwhelmed. The sense she had now was indescribable—it wasn't lust or passion, but something else she didn't have the right to feel in a "no strings" relationship. Her emotions right now made her think of a future with this *lawyer*, and that wasn't in the cards.

"I think I'm falling in love with you," he whispered into her hair, his breath moving the strands, tickling her scalp.

Sophie pulled herself up abruptly. She darted her gaze everywhere but in his direction. If she looked into his eyes, she would see a reflection of his feelings. She didn't want this from him. She didn't want this from anyone. She shook her head, more vigorously every second. When she pulled away this time, he let her go. She stalked across the yard, leaning against the side of the garage. After a long moment, he joined her, leaning his shoulder against the wood siding.

"I'm sorry," she said because she couldn't say what she thought he wanted to hear.

He pushed her sunglasses up and leaned forward, kissing her with tenderness, warmth, and love.

"Don't be sorry. I didn't tell you how I felt because I had any particular expectations. I just needed you to know how I feel about you. All I want is that we can keep seeing each other. I don't want to spend my nights without you."

Women got it all wrong. Lust was a lot easier than love. It was a pure, clean feeling with no expectations. He might think he was in love, but she was definitely in lust. She grabbed his face and kissed him hard, as she wanted to be kissed, a frenzied mating of lips and tongues. She snaked her hands under his maroon knit polo, loving the smooth warm skin pulled tight over the corded muscles of his back and the smooth plane of his chest, but she couldn't get enough. She put her hands into the oversized pockets of his cargo shorts, caressing his erection through the cloth.

He pulled his mouth from hers, his breathing labored. "We need to finish this inside."

By the time they'd completed the short walk from the back yard to her bedroom, neither had a stitch of clothing left.

She wanted to give him pleasure. Blindly, she sank to her knees, lightly scraping her fingers down his chest as she went. She wrapped her hand around him, and sucked his cock into her mouth, loving the taste, the texture, the feel of this man. She pulled at him with her lips and swirled against the head with her tongue, feeling his hips jerk involuntarily with almost every movement. She moved her other hand up his thigh enjoying the friction of the light dusting of blond hairs, and fondled his balls as gently as she could. He almost came apart at that moment.

He pulled her up. "Sunflower, I'm going to come too fast if you keep it up. Let me..." He paused, stroking her hair from her face. "Let me make love to you."

Just when she thought she'd put the past behind her, her nervousness and fear returned fourfold. She'd have been all right if he just wanted to fuck her. *Make love* seemed more intimate somehow.

His hands sliding down her chest and probing her center brought her attention squarely back to the moment. He pushed first one finger into her, finding her slickness. Another followed. When he kneeled before her, she felt suddenly boneless, and fell forward using his wide shoulders to brace herself.

She was glad for the support when he pressed his face against her trimmed curls, and blew a breath against her sex. He hadn't even touched the center of her and she felt like her heart was going to stop. Sex couldn't kill a person, right? He pushed his head deeper between her thighs, using his tongue to lap against the sensitive skin of her nether lips. His fingers made love to her, pressing against the nerve bundle on her inner wall. Then he sucked the swollen bud of her clitoris between his lips, flickering his tongue back and forth across the sensitive nub.

Her orgasm hit her like a tidal wave. She gasped his name over and over as a flood of pleasure rolled over her. He retreated slowly, pulling her down to the floor for a deep kiss. Her smell and taste surrounded them, enveloping them in the heady musk of great sex.

She pushed him onto the solid oak planks, and pulled

a condom from the bedside table, sheathing him first in latex, then with her sex as she took him in one deep plunge. He grabbed her hips and they found a rhythm that was hard and fast and suited them both.

Ryan pulsed inside her as he shouted upon his release, and Sophie was surprised to feel a smaller second orgasm hit her at that same moment. She fell forward onto his chest, their hearts beating in unison. After a few long minutes, he started caressing her back lazily.

"You're an amazing woman," he said, the timbre of his deep voice vibrating against her chest. His hand stopped the lazy circles he had been drawing on her back and came to rest against her hip, embracing her. He might as well have said those three little words again, the tone of his voice was such that she heard them anyway in everything he said.

She eased herself from him and started to stand. He caught her hand and looked at her, his eyes serious. "I love you," he said again with finality. The look in his eyes made her look away.

"Let me get this pink stuff out of my hair. Maybe we can do something fun with what's left of the weekend," she said flippantly over her shoulder. She closed the bathroom door and sank down on the closed toilet seat. What in the hell had she gotten herself into? She turned the shower on full blast. Steamy air fogged the mirrors. Happy she couldn't see her own expression, she stepped into the scalding shower.

· · ·

RYAN HAD JUST FINISHED CLEANING up in the guest bathroom and was zipping his cargo shorts when Sasha barked. The doorbell pealed a second time before the sound registered. He looked back toward the bedroom and listened—the shower was still going. Well, he'd just have to answer it.

He opened the door to reveal a striking blonde, impeccably dressed. Without a shirt, he suddenly felt very exposed.

She gasped, but quickly regained her composure. Her hand shot out to shake his.

"I'm Sophie's sister, Selena. And you are…" she trailed off expectantly.

"Ryan Becker." Remembering his manners, he shook her hand. "Nice to meet you. Why don't you come in and let me go put a shirt on," he said, spying his red knit polo dangling from the edge of the coffee table like a matador's cape. Suddenly, he saw what she would see first and scooped up their various clothes scattered around the room haphazardly and sprinted to the bedroom. "Sophie's in the shower. She'll…I'll, um, let her know you're here," he tossed over his shoulder.

Selie smirked. "I'll just make myself right at home."

Sophie was toweling her hair dry when Ryan slammed the door and unceremoniously dropped their clothes on the unused bed. "Your sister is here," he announced.

Sophie closed her eyes for a long moment. She slowly lifted her lashes, looking at him, resigned. "I gather you've already met her," she said, looking down at his bare chest. He nodded, rubbing a hand across his pecs self-consciously. "Great. Okay. Well." She exhaled a long breath. "Let's just get this over with." She pointed her small index finger at him. "You, put on a shirt and charm her. I'll get dressed." She shook her head. "It's just one big family reunion today, isn't it?"

Ryan emerged, fully dressed, every hair in place, this time the confident attorney. Selie had poured herself a glass of ice water with a slice of lemon. She was sitting at the dining room table flipping through a fashion magazine. She must have brought it with her. He'd never seen a magazine in Sophie's house. "Sorry about that earlier. It's nice to meet you," he said, shaking her hand yet again and settling in a chair across from her. "Sophie's told me a lot about you."

Selie looked up from her reading and glanced at him pointedly, her blue eyes cool. "I'm sorry, I can't say the same."

Spying the dog, Ryan scooped her up. "Have you met Sasha?" Selie gave the dog a couple of quick cursory pats. Clearly, she wasn't the dog lover in their family. "We found her on the one-oh-one—that's how Sophie and I met." He put the dog back on the floor and Sasha went back to her survey of the floor looking for whatever it was dogs looked for.

Selie's eyes sparkled with interest. "So...you're the suit. Then I can say, Sophie's told me a little about you too. Tell me you're not a lawyer."

What was it about the Reids and "suits"? He had an honest job like so many other people. They acted like he ate kittens for lunch. Ryan glanced over to the bedroom, hoping Sophie was coming out soon to save him from this odd conversation.

"I am. I'm in the corporate department at Equia." Turned out Selena knew several of his attorney colleagues and they talked a little shop, Ryan feeling far more comfortable on this topic.

Sophie finally emerged from the bedroom, hair gelled severely, in full gothic makeup, dark eyes and lips, and with a ring in every body piercing. She had become so natural with him that he'd forgotten about this particular armor she wore.

She hugged her sister around the neck quickly. Ryan could see the resemblance between the women. He would agree that Selena was more of a classic beauty, but he found Sophie's clear gray eyes and red-gold hair far more alluring. "What in the heck brings you by?" Sophie asked before settling across the dining room table, arms wrapped around her knees, bare feet propped on the chair cushions.

Selie smirked knowingly. She quirked an eyebrow the same way Sophie did. "You weren't answering your phone all weekend."

"We were in Big Bear, hiking and stuff. I just turned it off." She looked around the very quiet house. "Where's Madeline?"

"She's at home with Rob. She needs all the daddy daughter time she can get."

"Mmmm hmm." Sophie nodded. They looked at each other communicating without words from years of practice. "No, I'm not doing it."

"C'mon. You don't have to *do* anything. I'll just put both our names on the invitations and all you have to do is show up a little early. I thought we decided it was time."

The silence stretched between them again. Ryan looked back and forth between the sisters, their faces both stubbornly set.

"I hate to butt in, but what are you guys talking about?"

Selena patiently explained their father's lifetime achievement award from the bar association and the party their mother wanted them to host.

"I think you should do it," Ryan said unequivocally.

Selie smiled. "I agree with your boyfriend here. He's a smart one, a definite keeper."

"He's not...we're not..." Sophie protested.

Ryan tried not to visibly react to her words, though they stung. He thought they *were* something to each other after this weekend. But if she didn't think so, that was another conversation for another time. Definitely not something they should talk about in front of her sister.

Selie appeared to be looking meaningfully at something, and Ryan and Sophie both looked in the direction in which she was staring. Ryan had left Sophie's underwear hanging from the tall stool abutting the kitchen during his speedy clean up. He stood and grabbed for the white cotton briefs before stuffing them in his pocket.

"I must have misunderstood. I just assumed..." Selie trailed off.

SOPHIE WISHED FERVENTLY that she was in a cartoon and could use a pencil to draw a trap door that would open in the floor and swallow her whole. "If you can promise me it won't be an entire evening of them talking about what I should *really* be doing with my life, I'll do it. Get Mom to promise me that, and that she'll run interference with Dad and I'm on board." She banged her hand on the table with finality. "Those are my conditions. Plus they will not say *anything* about how I'm dressed."

"Deal." Selie stuck out her hand across the table and Sophie shook it. "I'll make sure Mom agrees. I'll e-mail you the details. It'll either be at the club or their house, we haven't decided, but it'll be formal."

"Of course. They wouldn't have it any other way." Her family acted like they were from prim and proper Boston, not laid back California. But she'd learned a long time ago it was best to go along.

Selie looked at her slim diamond and platinum watch. "Hey, I've gotta go before Maddy convinces her father to buy her a pony. Walk me to my car, sis."

It was so obvious her sister wanted to quiz her on the semi-dressed man who had appeared in the living room. Selie leaned against her Mercedes E-Class sedan, the car so clean that she was not worried about getting a speck of dirt on her white polo dress. Sliding her fashionably oversized glasses down her nose, she pierced Sophie with her blue eyes.

"A little stove-top stuffing?"

"You are not funny."

"So?"

"It's just a little fling."

"With a suit? This is so out of character for you, I don't know whether to applaud or have you committed."

"A girl's got needs, and can't always be picky."

"You should bring him. Mom and Dad would love him."

Sophie gagged. "I'll be there *alone*. No need to subject him to their scrutiny. It's not like we're serious or anything."

"He looked serious."

"He looked half-naked."

"Mmmm." Her sister nodded non-committally. "I'll e-mail you. You should come by and see Maddy one of these days. She loves you, you know."

"Yeah, quirky aunt and all that. I'll definitely stop by if I'm off this week. I know I don't always show it, but I love being her aunt. I miss her too."

She hugged her sister, more heartfelt this time. Selie pulled away and Ryan came down the walkway with the phone pressed to his ear.

"I have to go," he mouthed, while yessing the person on the other end of the phone.

Suddenly cold, despite the warm weather, Sophie hugged herself. Ryan gave her a brief, distracted kiss, and slid into his car. He waved, preoccupied, then pulled away from the curb.

Walking toward the house, Sophie rubbed at the goose bumps along her arms. The sex was great. Really, really great when she relaxed. So why did no-strings sex leave her feeling so bereft?

ELEVEN

STRIKE. One word dominated print and television news. The Sunday night TV anchors spun hair-raising tales of the effects a strike by the I.A.T.S.E. could have on the industry and local economy. If productions shut down, they warned, thousands of local residents could lose their jobs and the metropolitan economy billions of dollars.

Sophie was deeply ashamed of herself for neglecting the business side of her job. Caught up in the whirlwind of sex and screaming orgasms with Ryan, she hadn't been keeping on top of what was going on right in her own backyard. Okay, she'd definitely been on top of Ryan after an episode in the backyard. But she hadn't been keeping an eye on industry gossip or the trades. Despite the dire predictions from the press, she wasn't too worried about an imminent strike.

Every union in Hollywood renegotiated their contracts every three or four years—the writers, the directors, the actors, even the Teamsters. Strikes rarely happened. When contracts were set to expire, the local news stations rehashed the same old sensationalist stories on what a strike could mean to the local economy. At the last minute both sides met at the bargaining table, hashed out, and signed a new contract very much like the old one. Almost always.

Her phone rang, shaking her from her reverie. Maybe she needed a new ringtone. This damned Snoop Dogg was going to give her a heart attack.

"Hey, Sam," she said, eyeing the caller ID. She tried not to sound let down.

"I've been trying to get a hold of you since Friday. You haven't been answering."

Sophie had turned off her phone in order to focus completely on Ryan and his promise to make it a weekend she would remember. Too bad *he* hadn't blocked out the outside world. They could be together right now, making up for a lifetime of missed orgasms.

"You're still not answering now," Sam said, jarring her into the present.

"Sorry. What's going on?"

"Umm. The strike, Sophie. Have you watched the news, looked at the papers? I know we were sort of joking about it a few weeks ago, but it looks like it's really going to happen this time. Our contract expires at midnight —*tonight*. I'm hearing that we won't have to show up for calls on Monday. I've talked to a bunch of people and they're really worried about putting food on the table or making it through the holiday season without a paycheck."

"Let's not jump to conclusions until we get the skinny. Has local 706 called a meeting?" she asked, attempting to soothe Sam's fears. The last thing she wanted was a bunch of frenzied co-workers on her hands—when they had no individual decision making power. "Even though the union has strike authorization, the leadership promised they'd come back to us to get our input on whether to strike."

"I understand all that. But that doesn't mean I'm not a lot worried," Sam was working himself up, on the edge of hysteria. It was a sad day when she was the coolest head in a group of artists.

"Look, let me see what I can find out. Can you wait until tomorrow morning?"

"I don't think I can sleep. Can you call me back as soon as you find out anything, no matter what the time?"

Sophie agreed, ending the call.

Months ago, she'd taken on the task of strike captain, should negotiations falter. She scrounged through the pile of call sheets, make up, and art supply catalogues on her desk, until she found the phone tree for Local 706 and made a few calls. The good news was that she wasn't too late. Union reps had been calling everyone but hadn't gotten to the R's yet. A strike vote meeting started in a couple of hours.

The auditorium was buzzing with frenetic activity when Sophie eased her way down a crowded row to the one available seat she could find. The meeting started out with a slick, music enhanced PowerPoint presentation of all the demands the union was making: pay keeping pace with inflation, limiting the number of hours a studio could demand from them, and requiring larger contributions to cover ever escalating healthcare costs. From the murmurs of assent, it was clear that everyone agreed with the union's agenda.

Disagreements started when it was time to decide how to reach those goals. About half the members were ready to put down their brushes, pick up their placards, and strike. They vowed to push the producers and studios to the wall, holding out for the best possible deal, no matter how long they had to strike or what they had to sacrifice to get it. The other half were ready to compromise or do whatever it took to stay on the job and keep the paychecks coming in.

The meeting lasted long into the night, but after a lot of discussion and some yelling, the first group won out. Though it was past three o'clock in the morning, Sophie stayed after most members left, meeting with leadership. They briefed her on the job of strike captain, and she left at four determined to snatch a couple of hours of sleep before her strike duties started at eight on Monday morning.

She'd volunteered to captain a daily four hour shift rotating weekly between studios on the Westside, in Hollywood, and in the Valley. The union assigned her to Equia first. Some sleepless union volunteer delivered signs to her doorstep, and she put them in her back seat before she took off. After a trip to her favorite coffee shop for a triple shot pumpkin flavored cappuccino, she crawled down the 405 in her car and arrived at Equia's gates at eight o'clock for her first picket line.

Sophie led the small crowd in chanting the best protest she could create on the spot.

For the first two hours, they yelled, "What do we

want? Health care! When do we want it? Now!" The last two hours she switched to, "Put down your brushes! Pick up a sign!"

They weren't great, but that was why she wasn't a writer. The Writer's Guild slogans had been much better during their last strike.

To some extent, the other unions were honoring their strike and not crossing the picket lines. The suits, however, were driving through as if she and her fellow strikers weren't there at all. She'd stepped out of the line to chug another coffee someone had brought when a sleek Acura pulled up to the studio's guard gate. Whether her stomach plummeted because she was thinking about their nights together or her shock that he would dare cross her line and think he could hop in her bed later, she didn't know.

Though the armed guard was advancing upon her—they weren't allowed to interact with those crossing the picket line—she couldn't help herself.

The tinted window glided down silently, and a sunglass-wearing Ryan appeared. She saw his golden hair first, his obscured eyes next, then the sexy mouth.

"Lady, you're gonna have to move back," the guard said, one hand on his baton, the other on his gun. His badge identified him as Sean O'Rourke, deputy chief of Equia security.

"It's okay, O'Rourke," Ryan said to the guard. "I know her."

"You're crossing the line?" she asked, incredulous.

"It's my job. I've got no choice," he said bluntly. Then his demeanor softened. "I'm a lawyer, not studio management or a producer," he explained. "How are you doing? You okay?"

"I'm fine. I don't think the strike will go on too long." She gave him the same pat response she had given Selie and Holly. Truth was, she was scared she wouldn't be able to hold out more than a month or two without seeking help from her family. She would hate to do that after all her years of self-sufficiency. Sophie glanced at the cars lining up behind him, honking their horns. "Well, if you're going to go in, I guess you should go," she said, resigned.

He looked like he wanted to say something else. Instead, the window slid up as soundlessly as it had come down, and his car moved through the gate.

"Who's that guy?" one of the picketers asked.

"You friendly with the suits?" another said.

"He's a friend of a friend," she lied. She knew she should tell the truth, but she had a reputation to maintain with her colleagues. It had taken her a long time to earn their trust after they discovered she wasn't from a hardscrabble background. She had to work with these people every day on different sets. By admitting to a relationship with Ryan, they might think she was abandoning their cause.

She was handing over her sign and debriefing the afternoon strike captain when her phone blared "Sexual Seduction." Maybe a Bach concerto would be less jarring. She vowed to download a better ringtone when she got home.

"Come to lunch with me." Ryan said without preamble. It wasn't a question. It was a command.

She didn't like dictators. "I'm tired. I didn't get a lot of sleep. I have to go home and let Sasha out," she told him.

"I'll meet you in twenty minutes at Craft," he said, naming an upscale restaurant in Century City, before disconnecting the call.

The…*gall!* The unmitigated gall! Sophie had half a mind not to show up. That would show him. She was determinedly driving along the San Diego freeway north toward the Valley when she found herself exiting at Santa Monica Boulevard. She pulled up to the restaurant on Constellation Boulevard and handed her keys and handed off her car to the man in the red vest and bowtie in exchange for a flimsy claim ticket.

Damned car culture. It would serve her right if someone drove away with her car one day. She looked into the half-empty restaurant and spotted Ryan, his nimble thumbs flying across the Blackberry keys. Well maybe she hadn't stood him up, but he would surely pay. She was ravenous and would happily have an appetizer, an entrée, and a dessert on his tab.

She pulled the brim on her baseball cap low and pushed her bug-eyed glasses all the way up her small nose, celebrity style. She ignored the exquisitely turned out patrons who sniffed at her t-shirt and shorts. Let them think she was a devil-may-care celeb. It was far better than having a fellow striker from nearby Fox studios recognize her as what she was—a traitor.

. . .

EVEN WITH MOST of her face covered and her red-gold hair spilling helter-skelter from her baseball cap, she was enchanting.

Remembering his manners, Ryan stood when she approached the table. "I didn't think you'd come," he said as they both sat.

She picked up the menu, pulling off her glasses to study the offering. "I didn't plan to, but I thought I should explain to you why we're on strike."

"Sophie, I know why you're on strike. The same reason any union goes on strike: to get more from so-called 'management,'" he said, making air quotes with his fingers. "Whether the more is more money, more vacation time, or more health care doesn't matter."

Her face grew red with barely suppressed indignation. He checked himself. Now would probably not be the time to mention that she looked sexy as hell or put her hand on his growing erection, though he would love to see her fierce eyes go soft and her jaw grow slack as he stroked the anger from her body.

"Ryan, this is my livelihood. It does matter." She began, her escalating voice unchecked. "Housing prices, gas prices, food prices, everything is astronomical here in L.A. My fellow union members are trying to raise kids in and around the city. Movie ticket prices go up, DVDs are selling like hotcakes, and cable is exploding. We deserve a cut of that pie. Without us, the show couldn't go on. Have you ever seen an actor without make-up? With their hair scraped back in a greasy ponytail?"

He nodded, though unadorned celebrities were not forefront in his thoughts. Her face, sans make up, with her hair naturally soft and curly, waking from sleep, flushed with passion beneath him, flashed in his mind. *She* looked just fine without makeup—just creamy skin and freckles.

"Without us they couldn't prance down the red carpet looking like a million bucks or do magazine spreads, much less high-definition close ups. They'd look like they do in those horrible tabloid photos." She wrinkled her cute little nose in disgust. "Without us, it kind of ruins the fantasy."

He nodded again, trying to focus on what she said and not how kissable her lips looked. She paused when their server approached the table. He ordered a beet and goat cheese salad, then threw caution to the wind and got a steak. Sophie ordered several oysters to start and the twenty-nine dollar imported Hawaiian blue prawns.

Ryan tried to listen as she talked about health care, pensions, and retirement and the future of unions in the world. He really, really tried. He was sure he caught some things she said in between her pursed lips slurping oysters like a pro, her tongue darting out to catch the Tabasco sauce that caught in the corner. She ate her shrimp with the same enthusiasm, butter and lemon dripping from her fingers. Before she could pick up a napkin, he gave into impulse and pulled her buttery index finger into his mouth, sucking the sweet liquid off slowly.

Sophie pulled her finger back as if she'd been singed by fire. Her rapid breathing and budding nipples belied her words.

"I can't believe you did that. We're having a serious discussion here."

If she were a cartoon character, steam would have been coming out of her ears.

"But you're really hot when you're passionate about something," he said honestly.

"Are you thinking about sex right now?"

He considered lying. It would probably be the best thing to do. Women wanted to talk, and men, well... talking about the union versus the Alliance of Motion Picture and Television Producers was not what he'd wanted to do when he saw her that morning, nor was *talking* what he wanted to do while sitting across the table from her now. All that schooling wouldn't go to waste. He chose evasion instead.

"I think it's a matter of the union deciding what's most important and going for that," he said instead of the other things he could have whispered into her ear.

"You didn't answer my other question," she said accusingly.

"I don't think you want me to answer that right now."

There was a long pause before she picked up where she'd left off.

"Ryan, I don't think we should compromise. Look what's happened to the other unions over the last few years. Once we give up one thing, who knows what else we'll have to give up?"

"Are they having problems getting workers to replace you?"

Sophie shook her head in grudging acknowledgement of his point. "No."

"You know from firsthand experience how hard it is getting into one of the Hollywood unions. There always going to be people who are willing to work for less, and you're competing against them, not the studios." In a far corner of his brain, he heard her, really he did, but her lips, still shiny with butter, were the focus of his gaze. She was still sexy when she passionately argued her union's position, but he didn't want to start something he couldn't finish. He did have to go back to work today, and he didn't want to have to concentrate on work with a raging hard-on chafing against his fly. When the blood rushed down, it made focusing on the tasks that required his other head difficult.

She finished off her shrimp and was eyeing the dessert menu when his phone vibrated against the table.

"I'm sorry."

"I know," she said. The buzzing persisted. "You have to get that."

It was the studio. The union had compromised on some of its demands and it was time to marshal their forces before they got back to the bargaining table. He hung up, and pushed his platinum card into the waiter's hand.

"I have to go. Things are really tense at work right now."

Sophie looked disappointed again. He hated that he put that look on her face. He liked the look of smug satisfaction she got after good sex much, much better. And he wanted to see a lot more if it.

She put down the dessert menu, gathered up her tote bag sized purse, and plopped her sunglasses back on her pert little nose.

"What's up at Equia that's keeping you there night and day?" she asked, genuine concern in her voice. He was thrilled that she took an interest in him as more than a convenient sex toy. He would like to share some of the burdens from work with her, but he cared too much, and desperately wanted to protect her from the ups and downs of the strike. He used attorney-client privilege as a false excuse again.

"Nothing much I can talk about. We're just negotiating some complicated deals right now and the studio bosses want everyone's nose to the grindstone twenty-four hours a day until everything is hashed out. You know how complicated it can get when everybody wants everything yesterday."

She nodded in understanding. "Well, I guess I'll see you around?"

It broke his heart that he had shaken her confidence in him, again.

When they got to the lobby, Ryan pulled her into a nook and took what he'd wanted all morning. He caught her by surprise, but then her lips opened for him. She tasted earthy, like his woman. He grabbed her ass, pulling her as close as their clothes would allow. She felt so good. He wanted to brand her, make her useless for anyone else. Embarrassed by his caveman thoughts and techniques, he pushed her away more abruptly than intended.

"Sorry, I have to go." He didn't know what had gotten into him, but he needed to clear his head. The little head was doing all the thinking when they were together, and the little head hadn't gone law school.

TWELVE

SOPHIE WAS SAVED by the bell. The blaring of her phone rescued them from an embarrassing moment. She didn't know what had gotten into Ryan, but he was acting weird. She stepped back into the lobby nook. "Private Number," the caller ID read.

The caller identified himself as Gregg Mackins, leader of the negotiating committee. Sophie was perplexed that someone so high up in the union would be calling her, a lowly strike captain. They agreed to meet for coffee in an hour or so near her house.

She ordered decaffeinated chai when she arrived for her meeting. Any more fully loaded coffee and her hair would stand on end, without gel. Gregg had described himself as a forty-year-old pudge. A dead ringer for Jason Alexander lounged at a back table with two other men and a woman she'd never met before. Introductions made, she slipped into the booth with her drink.

Gregg took the reins. "Sophie, first we want to thank you for agreeing to act as strike captain. You're doing a great job at Equia," he said, and following his lead the others fawned over her a few more minutes.

She'd only led chants, carried signs, and picked up coffee—nothing earth shattering. Her natural suspicion kicked in. "Why are you guys blowing smoke up my ass?"

Taken aback by her matter-of-fact question, guilty looks passed between Gregg and the others. He finally spoke. "We want you on NegCom."

"Why would you want me on the negotiating committee? I don't have any particular knowledge or expertise that you guys wouldn't have covered," she said, getting more suspicious by the moment.

One of the women spoke up impatiently. "We heard that your dad is Judge Harry Reid and your uncle is an ALJ with the NLRB, is that true?"

Heat stole through Sophie's face in frustration, not embarrassment. "Exactly. My *dad* is a federal judge and my *uncle* is an administrative law judge with the National Labor Relations Board. *I'm* just a makeup artist."

"Look, we want you there to help us intimidate them. We're not asking you to assert some kind of influence over your family or anything unethical like that. We just want to spread this info around to throw the other side off during the meeting tomorrow morning."

Gregg spoke up. "The studios have asked us to come in with our best and final offer. We're losing ground in these negotiations and need a little edge. Please. Say yes. Your opinion is as important as any other union member."

Sophie blew out a breath and sipped her cooling tea. Sometimes it seemed no matter what she did, she could not break away from her upbringing. After all she had done to break out, establish her own identity, be her own person, people still wanted that other Sophie Reid, the San Marino judge's daughter.

She stood, pulling her large bag with her. "Let me think about this. I'll call you later, Gregg."

After a well-deserved nap, Sophie retreated to her artist's studio. Since she'd met Ryan, she hadn't spent much time painting. Now, with the weight of the world on her shoulders, she needed the stress outlet working with oils provided.

She tuned the radio to a classical music station that wouldn't steal her focus. Cool blue walls soothed her as she examined the unfinished painting on the easel. It was a self-portrait of sorts. The main woman in the portrait wasn't reflective of her—it was anyone and everyone. Rather, each face in the hair of the painted woman reflected the range of emotions warring through her.

Family, work, her relationships with men all informed the little Sophies. She added three faces today. The first exemplified the tension between her past and present. The second was a woman shouting, passionate about her cause. She dropped her brush, and her heart thumped several times before she was able to draw the face in her imagination. The last small face was how she imagined herself in the midst of a Ryan initiated orgasm.

A knock on the door made her drop her brush again. Good thing she'd remembered the thick canvas drop cloth. The light knock sounded again. What in the hell? No one knew about the room back here, other than her realtor, and she knew that ball of energy wrapped in a gold blazer wouldn't drop by unannounced.

Covered in red, orange, and yellow paint, she pulled open the small door. Ryan stood there looking sexier than should be allowed, stubble shadowing his jaw.

"How did you..." The question died on her lips. This wasn't the playful man who teased her senses through lunch. Instead, the man who faced her looked like he needed comfort. As best she could, given her diminutive height, she pulled him into her arms, wrapping an arm around one broad shoulder, the other snaking around a lean waist. They stood like that for a long moment. Unwrapping herself, she said, "Go into the house. The back door is unlocked. Let me clean up my brushes and meet you in there."

Except for the dog's nails clicking along the wood floor, the house was as quiet and dark as a tomb when she entered. Ryan hadn't turned on the lights even though the sun had set while she was painting. If she hadn't seen his car was still in the driveway, she'd have thought Ryan had been an apparition appearing through her sheer force of will.

She smelled it before she saw it. Turning on a lamp, she noticed that Ryan must have brought over Indian take out. Mouthwatering garlic, ginger, and scents of curry permeated the dining room. The dog spun and jumped around the table looking a little too eager. She moved the food out of the pup's reach and ventured to the bedroom. Ryan was fast asleep, fully clothed on top of the bedspread.

His eyes flickered open when she crossed the thresh-old. She sat on the end of the bed taking in his conservative black silk socks. When had Brooks Brothers become sexy to her? "Please, make yourself at home."

"I know I didn't call. I had a beastly day, but I wanted to see you again." His blue gaze penetrated her.

Her eyes skidded away. "You brought dinner. You hungry?"

He nodded. "I hope you like curry. I picked it up from a place I like on Ventura."

"I'll be right back." She started for the door. "Oh, you might want to take off your suit and hang it in the closet or something if you don't want short blond dog hairs all over it."

"You can just admit you want me naked." His voice was both playful and suggestive. "I'll strip for you anytime."

Sophie rolled her eyes heavenward and went to get the food. She loaded up a thick wooden tray with tandoori chicken, lamb korma, bhindi masala, and warm, buttery naan and scooped it all up. When she came back with dinner, he'd stripped. His lightly tanned skin stood out against the stark white undershirt and pale blue boxers he still wore. She was dying to skim her hands along the fine blond hairs that dusted his arms and legs. Thank goodness she had iron control over her impulses. Accepting the tray on his lap, he draped a cloth napkin across his waist and picked up the knife and fork. She sat cross-legged across from him and nibbled at a little bread.

. . .

"TODAY WASN'T the first time you saw my studio." It was a statement, not a question. Her husky voice quavered with vulnerability.

He paused, dropping his utensils on the tray and wiping his mouth. He took a long drink of water before he answered. "I just happened upon it before we went to brunch with my family."

Sophie was quiet, too quiet for his taste. He wanted to tell her that she was brilliant and talented and that he would never breach her privacy again. But the last part would be a lie. He wanted to breach the protective shell she wore. He wanted her to be herself, whatever that was, when he was with her. He wanted to be involved in every part of her life.

"Not many people know I paint." Sophie ducked her head in embarrassment. "I just do it for me. My parents always said it was a silly hobby."

He felt honored to see a part of her few shared.

"I don't think it's silly," he said. "I think your work is beautiful. It's emotional and reflects what's in your heart. You should display it, if not at a gallery, at least in the house."

"Maybe one day," she said. "Well, I'd kind of appreciate it if you didn't go in there again. I need a space that's just my own."

The subject closed, they went back to the food. Eventually abandoning good manners, Ryan dropped the knife and ate with gusto. Halfway through the food on the shared plates, he noticed that she hadn't really eaten anything.

"Aren't you hungry from all that walking and shouting and sign waving?" he inquired.

Taking another small bite of her bread, she looked at him under heavy lidded eyes. "I had a big lunch."

SHE KNEW RIGHT THEN she should not have mentioned their noontime meal. She'd only wanted to express that trying to bankrupt him at lunch had left her full. But he wasn't interested in her stomach right now. Desire sparked in his eyes and he abandoned the supper, which had held such interest moments ago.

"Speaking of lunch, I think there's some unfinished business to attend to…"

He swung his legs over the edge of the bed and placed the tray on top of the dresser. Sasha stood on her hind legs and sniffed at the air around the chest of drawers.

Sophie stood too, scooting the dog toward the door. Ryan squeezed her upper arm, closing the door behind the dog with his foot. "The dog can wait. I can't."

The scents of old incense, fresh curry, and anticipation swirled around them. His lips brushed across hers and her token resistance to Ryan melted away. He began to kiss her in earnest, walking her over to the bed. They tumbled onto the plush duvet, the feathers enveloping them. Her paint-splattered shirt and old jeans hit the floor first. Even with her eyes closed, she knew Ryan's swift intake of breath came because she was braless. Clad only in sturdy underwear, Sophie turned inward, ready to submit to the pleasure his kisses promised. But he broke away before she could mindlessly succumb.

Suddenly, she felt bereft. She opened her eyes, surprised to see he was still in his underwear, his erection straining the fly of his boxers.

"I want to try something."

Her arousal-fogged brain cleared just a little bit. "What?" she asked, uncertain.

"Do you trust me?"

"Yes." She did. Implicitly. It was herself she didn't trust to not think of him when he was gone, because his leaving was inevitable. Men ran from Sophie. It was just what happened. She didn't trust herself to keep her heart in check, when he'd put his out there on the line. But there was no question that she trusted him.

He pulled the scarves from her lamps and used one to blindfold her. The other he used to lash her wrists together. When she started to protest, he placed a silencing finger on her lips.

"I don't want you to tense up thinking so much about what's going to happen next. I just want you to feel." He trailed his fingers lightly along her jaw, down the arch of her neck, to her narrow shoulder. She relaxed. This man knew how to play her body like a violin. Not coming was no longer on the forefront of her mind, feeling good was. "If you want to stop, or remove the blindfold, just let me know," he said, his voice serious. She nodded in acquiescence.

Without her sight, her other senses became infinitely more acute. She smelled the incense Ryan found in a drawer and lit, its pungent scent filling the room. She could hear him rustling around the room doing God knows what. Her skin rose in goose bumps, and her nipples beaded in anticipation.

A warm hand smoothed against her waist and she squeezed her thighs in anticipation.

"I'm going to strip your panties now." His husky voice commanded her to open her thighs and she felt the elastic and cotton scrape down her legs, leaving her completely bare to his gaze. She squirmed, knowing without seeing, that she was under his scrutiny.

The air stirred around her, lifting the fine hairs on her body.

She felt Ryan's hot, damp kiss on her neck before it registered. His next kiss landed on the arch of her foot, making her toes curl. His lips graced her slim calves, the backs of her knees, and her belly button—untraditional erogenous areas, yet his touch made her thighs slick with her own arousal. And he hadn't even touched her yet, not really. Not in those places that would send her into the stratosphere.

Then he did. His hot mouth and sexy lips covered her breast, his tongue playing against her nipple. She couldn't see now, but she could remember how his head had looked pressed against her paler chest. Her hips bucked off the bed when a single finger parted her nether lips and slicked ever so lightly over her clitoris. She cried his name involuntarily.

He laughed softly. "You want me to stop?"

"God, no," she replied, her breath catching as he used his thumb to stroke her clit again and again, just hard enough to make her sweat, but not hard enough to make her come. She'd never thought so before, but the edge of orgasm was a nice place to be.

His mouth fused with hers. Their tongues mated and retreated. As his weight settled onto her, she hooked a leg around his hip, opening herself to him. His erection nudged her hip and she twisted, trying to get closer to him, if that was possible.

"I want you," she said, pausing for a much-needed breath. She undulated under him, trying to spark in him the same sense of urgency she felt. "It feels like I've wanted you forever," she blurted out. Damn. Had she just said that? She couldn't even blame her outburst on alcohol.

"I've wanted this from almost the first moment I met you," he said, stroking her hair away from her face.

"What are you waiting for, Ryan? Make love to me." Not having to look into those piercing ocean blue eyes made it easier to admit that she wanted him as much as he apparently wanted her.

"Condom?" he asked, his voice hoarse.

"In the drawer," she said, then regretted it. She strained against her temporary bonds.

"Wait…" But she knew it was too late. She heard his surprised intake of breath and then listened to the crackle of cellophane as he unsealed the box and tore a packet from what was probably world's longest single strip of condoms.

"My little Sophie has surprised me yet." He covered her again, this time they were both naked and his hands and mouth were everywhere. Without sight, she couldn't follow where one touch ended or another began. A single finger probed her slickness, and then he was there, full and hard, pushing against her opening. She released her breath as he'd taught her, and let a wave of pleasure roll over her as he eased into her, inch by glorious inch. It was so hard to take all this pleasure and give nothing in return. She broke one of his rules and looped her bound wrists behind his neck. Ryan set a slow rocking rhythm that kept her on the edge of orgasm for what seemed like forever.

He grabbed her hips and she reflexively hooked her ankles around his waist, pushing her clit against the root of his cock. Each thrust was like a taste of heaven. He reached behind his head and unknotted and unwound the scarf binding her hands.

"Touch yourself for me," Ryan demanded. "Make yourself come."

Sophie was sure she turned as red as her hair. She'd never been an exhibitionist. Not really. Her bravado, her swaggering, and displays of courage were an act, pure and simple. It kept people from getting too close to the real her. First Ryan had seen her at her most vulnerable when she admitted to him that she was bad at sex. Then he'd seen her real hair color. He knew she was self-conscious about her large nipples. No matter how turned on she was, she didn't think she could be this on display for him.

She gripped his shoulders hard, glad that she couldn't see. "I don't think I can do this, Ryan." Couldn't he just fuck her hard and fast with no remorse?

She slid a free hand down his chest, across his hard pecs, and tweaked a small male nipple. He groaned, involuntarily distracted, his rhythm broken momentarily.

"Please trust me on this, Sophie."

Closing her eyes behind the scarf, she released his nipple and took her own between her thumb and finger, squeezing hard. The other hand she used to pinch the hard bud of her clit. The trio of sensations from her hands and his cock brought her to the edge again and again.

His breathing changed. "Are you close?" he asked. She could feel how close he was, how carefully he was holding himself back for her.

"Do it," he whispered near her ear. "Do this for yourself." And she did, touching herself in a way that she knew would bring her to climax, no longer self-conscious or worried about how she looked. It was glorious to be able to just feel. He rode her high and hard. Her orgasm hit her like a tidal wave, her insides clenching around his cock, milking his orgasm from him. He crushed her mouth again, their tongues dueling, both winning. He shouted his release into her, and she swallowed the breath, taking in the essence of him.

He pulled off her scarf, tossing it carelessly on the nightstand. He kissed each eyelid gently as he cupped her face. He looked like he wanted to say something, but he hesitated, quiet for a long moment. She thought she knew what he wanted to ask, so she blurted out what was on her mind.

"I've never used any of those condoms."

Ryan looked confused for a time, then he smiled. "I know, Sophie."

"I just bought them because it seemed like something a single girl should do."

She was babbling to cover her nervousness. She felt very vulnerable to Ryan after what had just happened between them. There was very little about her that he didn't know. It was both a comforting and scary feeling. It was like a homecoming and bungee jumping at the same time.

He eased from the bed, and after a quick trip to the bathroom, came back to bed, gathered her in his arms, and pulled the duvet over both of them.

"Thank you for trusting me. I only want to do what makes you feel good. I would never do anything to hurt you, ever," he said fiercely.

"I know, Ryan. You're just an honorable guy that way." Her tone was light, but she was serious. He was turning out to be an honorable guy who was coincidentally giving her the best orgasms of her life. With Ryan warm and sexy and tucked in under the covers, her mind drifted to the other big issue in her life — the strike.

"Can I ask your advice on something?"

"Hmmm," he said, getting more comfortable. Then he yawned. "Anything."

Sophie started talking about the strike and Gregg's request. When she didn't get an answer on whether she should join the NegCom at the table in the morning, she looked over only to see his eyes were closed and his chest slowly moving up and down with deep, even breaths. She really liked Ryan, but sometimes he was just a typical man. Naked and satisfied, he was snoring lightly in her bed, oblivious to everything around him.

Good thing she didn't need hours of cuddling. She was learning that trusting a man didn't have to mean giving over all her power. She knew that she needed to trust herself more too. She'd gone with her gut with Ryan against her better judgment, and that was working out fine. A sex buddy without commitment was just what she had needed to boost her confidence in the bedroom.

She needed that boost in her professional life as well. If she were more assertive, maybe she could have it all. She just needed to go after what she wanted. And what she wanted now, what she believed in with all her heart, was that the union was at a crucial turning point in history. They needed to win all the concessions they could from the studios at whatever cost. As long as what they went about it in a fair way.

Intellectually, she knew that she would not become a carbon copy of her money and image-obsessed parents if she admitted she was related to them. It was time to get her emotions on board. The union's goals were important to her, and if she had to trade on her good name to get her friends and colleagues what they deserved, then so be it. She tiptoed out of the room, careful not to disturb Ryan, and grabbed her cell. Watching Sasha chase a chipmunk across the backyard, she dialed Gregg's number.

RYAN WAS BONE WEARY. Working from dawn to dusk then slipping over to Sophie's for a not-so-quick romp had been a bad idea for his health. His unshaven face, wrinkled shirt, and bloodshot eyes were not a pretty sight. Co-workers who had never seen him less than impeccable were taking the opportunity to poke fun at the obvious addition of a woman, or a really bad recreational drug habit, to his life.

They were back at the same mile-long conference

table. The studio lawyers and producers' representatives sat along the window side making last minute decisions. The other side of the table was empty save for thick negotiation packets placed on the leather placemats before each chair. Negotiating postures set, they took a ten-minute break. It was nine fifty and the union negotiating committee was scheduled to be here promptly at ten A.M.

Ryan was staring out at the ocean when Mitchell Riley sauntered up to him. He groaned inwardly.

"Hey, man, you must be gettin' some the way you rolled in here this morning," Mitch said, waggling his eyebrows.

Ryan smiled slightly, but didn't answer. His relationship with Sophie was not for public consumption.

Mitchell punched him lightly on the shoulder. "Is she a sexy brunette like that last girl you went out with? Josie something..." he said, snapping his fingers trying to remember.

"No, she's a redhead, actually." Ryan could have kicked himself for rising to the bait. Mitch was like a terrier, though, and wouldn't let go until you gave him a little something.

"Feisty, huh? That's a change. You bringing her to happy hour next week?" Every month or so, the lawyers in his department, and sometimes their significant others, got together for wine and tapas at a local bar. Practicing law, even in a place as big as this, was a solitary activity. The get-togethers gave them an off-the-clock opportunity to socialize and relax together. Their department head, the assistant general counsel, was always there. The parties weren't exactly mandatory, but no one missed more than one or two a year.

"Maybe. I'll be sure to ask Sophie."

"Sophie, huh? That's gotta be a pretty unique name."

"I guess…" Ryan said, not following Mitch.

"I'm just sayin', man. I was looking at the list of NegCom members and there was a Sophie Reid on there. I hear she's connected—father and uncle are judges. Uncle's on the NLRB. She may wipe the floor—"

Ryan was back at his chair in a shot, flipping through the thick stack. Finding the right page, he ran his finger down the names until he saw it in black and white. Sophie Reid. He didn't have time to think or figure out what to do because as soon as he dropped the papers back on the table with a resounding thunk, the union negotiators entered. He saw her red-gold hair, pulled into a severe ponytail, before she saw him. Life slowed like it did on television before the inevitable collision scene. He knew the moment she looked up and saw him. She lost her composure for just a moment, her eyes distrustful, where last night there had been faith.

THIRTEEN

RYAN'S INPUT at the meeting was negligible. Mitch might have been a lot of things—a loudmouth, annoying, nosy, pushy jerk—but he was an excellent lawyer. Once Mitch realized that Ryan was down for the count, he picked up the slack for the both of them.

Instead of taking notes, he spent much of the first two hours staring at Sophie. Who could have tricked her into coming here? She was an honest person and a straight shooter. She, of all people, would never trade on her family name for gain. More than any other woman he had ever met, she understood the value of standing on her own and earning everything she had the old fashioned way, with hard work and perseverance. She'd proven that a person could do well even in the face of adversity, and he was immensely proud of her, loved her for those qualities he held so dear.

Both sides were progressing on a number of issues. But they were still at loggerheads on the issue of studio and producer contributions to the union's retirement fund when the moderator called for a ten-minute break. A group of people immediately surrounded Sophie, including a man who touched her far too often and too intimately for Ryan's taste and a couple of women he'd seen at the negotiating table during other meetings. They finally broke their animated discussion and he was able to pull her aside to snatch a few seconds with her.

"What in the hell are you doing here?" he hissed, probably too harshly. "And who is that guy with his hands all over you?"

"That *guy*—Gregg—asked me to be on the committee, and I thought it was the least I could do," she said.

"Sophie, you have to know that they're using you. It's not your expertise they want you here for," he whispered when he realized others on the committee were watching them with interest. "Unions can't be trusted blindly."

The moderator cleared his throat and a few people shuffled back to their seats, closed their cell phones, and put PDAs in pockets.

"What do you mean? I know exactly why I'm here, Ryan," she said, starting to sound exasperated.

He obviously wasn't explaining himself well. He had to communicate to her that the union was using her in the worst way. She would be devastated when she found out, but he knew he'd be there for any fallout.

He lowered his voice still more, and she had to lean in closer to hear him. "Before the meeting, your *friends* over there circulated information about your dad and uncle." Her eyes widened, and he was relieved she finally got it. "I'm sorry that you had to hear it this way—"

She cut him off. "I know *that*, Ryan. It was the least I could do."

The flush of anger rose high on his cheekbones. How could she come on his turf, wielding all sorts of influence, but fail to mention it to him? He was about to quiz her on those exact issues of openness and trust, but the moderator firmly requested that everyone return to their seats for another negotiating session.

Ryan was in top form this time around. He argued, yelled, and pressed the position of his clients, the movie studios, until the union backed down on certain issues. The committee argued long into the night. Ryan did not get another chance to talk to Sophie alone. Union members crowded around her during every break.

The committee had made a tentative agreement on every issue but one. Ryan insisted they take one last break so they could bring in coffee and some food. Then, fortified, they could get to the final issue. He might not be able to talk to Sophie, but he thought of one way to get her attention. He pulled out his Blackberry and sent her a text message. *"Is someone looking after Sasha today?"*

When the phone buzzed in her hand, she pulled away from the group and flipped open the top. She read the message and slid her gray eyes over to him, the expression in them unreadable. But she texted him back. *"My neighbors have her at their house."*

He sent her one more message. *"Can I come over later?"*

"Fine," she replied.

Satisfied with the response, he shoved the Blackberry into his pocket.

Sasha was in good hands, and he'd be at her place

later. No matter how misguided her motives, he would be able to forgive her after he explained where she'd gone wrong. He knew she'd see it his way, and then they could get on with carving out some kind of relationship. If the union and studios were able to reach a deal tonight, he probably wouldn't be back at the negotiating table, with this union for years at least, until this contract expired.

During the long break, opposing sides exchanged pleasantries, and some of the hairdressers shared tales of the biggest stars, making everyone laugh and putting everybody in a jovial mood. The shot of caffeine no doubt helped the mood as well. The group returned to the table refreshed.

The moderator cleared his throat. He used a laser pointer to draw everyone's attention to the blackboard mounted at the far end of the conference room.

"We've reached a tentative agreement on the first six points on the board," he said, highlighting each with the red light of the pointer. The last and only issue we need to address are AMPTP residual payments to the health and pension funds.

"Ryan, why don't you go first?" the moderator said. "What is AMPTP's position?"

He cleared his throat, deliberately averting his eyes from Sophie. He pointedly looked at everyone else around the room.

"Look, the pension and health benefits that I.A.T.S.E. union members enjoy are better than most Americans'. Local 706 members can qualify for comprehensive bene-fits for themselves and their families with less than two months of full time work. Health costs are skyrocketing across the board. We'll do our part to shoulder those increases, but ask that union members share in that burden.

"Our direct and residual contributions to the union's retirement fund average six hundred million a year, and this amount climbs annually. Employees add zero. Currently there is no standard for payments based upon new media content. The future of Internet content is too speculative for us to agree to a framework of contribution. We'd like to defer it three years until the next contract. Thank you."

Mitch gave Ryan a surreptitious thumbs up sign. The moderator looked over to the other side of the table. Ryan hoped his jaw did not drop when Sophie began to speak. She'd been quiet during all of the early hours of the negotiation.

"My name is Sophie Reid and I'm a makeup artist and a union member," she started. Obviously not used to public speaking, she cleared her throat, and nervously looked down at the prepared statement. "Like many other union members, I make a living exclusively from work on television shows, movies and commercials. I live in Southern California, one of the most expensive areas of the country. I stay here because my family is here and because I love my job.

"In the last few years, costs have skyrocketed. Housing has increased over 200 percent, and health care costs are not far behind. The costs of food, gas, and other necessities have increased in tandem.

"We're only asking for our fair share of the millions of dollars producers and studios make as a result of our work. That means payment for footage, no matter where it's used. That also means increased payments for health-care and retirement so union members don't have to shoulder the cost. We don't want to go bankrupt now from sudden catastrophic illness or later from an under-funded retirement. Thank you."

Ryan shook his head, amazed that Sophie was involved with these people.

He looked directly at her when he spoke. "Wouldn't you rather have this residual money in your pocket? History is fraught with unions squandering pension money. If the union members have the dollars in their pocket, then you all can invest it responsibly, like workers in many other industries do with their 401k plans."

Gregg broke in. "Mr. Becker, I resent your implica-tion. Our union is not enriching itself at the expense of its members."

Ryan shuffled through the stack before him before brandishing the offending document. "Then why has the union pension underperformed in the stock market for the last five years? Sophie or anyone could do better investing in a garden variety index fund."

"Every fund manager has good years and bad years," Gregg countered.

"That may be true, Mr. Mackins, but if you have many more bad years, you'll be back in our pocket looking for us to make up the difference."

"*I* wouldn't ask you or anyone for money," Sophie said. "Fluctuating stock performances shouldn't scare us. The benefits of being in the union far outweigh the detriments."

"That's your sense of entitlement speaking."

The look she gave him could have frozen water. "We're not asking for a handout. We're asking for our fair share of what we earn for you. Without us, you would have actors on screen looking as bad as their tabloid photos. Who would watch your shows then? It's difficult to believe a twenty-five-year-old with bad acne is a super popular sixteen-year-old teenager without good hair and makeup."

Voices rose and sparks flew—Sophie's and Ryan's two of the loudest. AMPTP members argued that union members wanted benefits in a climate where employers offered these benefits to fewer and fewer workers. Local 706 members thought the producers and studios were money hungry, trying to keep the proceeds of an exploding DVD and Internet market to themselves.

Once she got into the groove, Sophie argued no less vociferously than her union cohorts. Sparked by anger, or competition, Ryan did the same. An hour in, the moderator blew a whistle, startling everyone into silence.

"I don't know what exactly is going on here, but you're arguing, even though you're only a few dollars apart. Please choose one person from your group to speak. And in my opinion as your moderator, that person should not be Sophie Reid nor Ryan Becker."

Sophie turned as red as her hair. Ryan glared at the moderator, but a stiff hand on his arm from Mitch helped him keep his mouth shut. And the moderator was right— after he and Sophie got out of the discussion, the group was able to hash out a tentative agreement on the final points within half an hour.

"After the respective representatives take the agreements back to their members for a vote, we'll agree to meet back here in five days and set a date for a tentative signing ceremony," the moderator said. He closed by thanking each member of the committee, personally shaking each and every person's hand.

Everyone looked as exhausted as Ryan felt, and despite his simmering anger, he wanted nothing more than to spend the last few hours of the night with his arms around Sophie. When he caught up with her in the parking lot, though, she had other ideas.

"I'm going home, Ryan. Alone." Clearly, she was still angry. They were on the ground floor of the indoor parking lot. She pointed the key fob at her yellow car. The doors unlocked with an electronic beep.

"I think we should talk," he said. Then, noticing the others around them walking to their cars, he lowered his voice. "But not here."

"I'm not going to your house and you're not coming to mine, so if you have something to say, this is your chance." She tapped her foot impatiently.

"Fine," he said, walking to his car, their public discussion over.

SHE WASN'T surprised when he pulled up behind her in her driveway. She ignored him, walked into the house, and greeted the dog who was sleepy but excited. She could have told Ryan he wasn't wanted. She could have locked the door. But she wanted him to follow.

Sophie let Sasha out back, and Ryan was waiting for

her, sans tie but otherwise still very buttoned up in his navy pinstripe suit, when she came back to the house. He stood leaning against the kitchen counter, arms crossed, breathing hard. Despite the anger radiating from him, he was still sexier than he had any right to be. And she wanted to smack herself upside the head for even thinking about how attractive he was in the present mood. She wanted to kiss him or kick him, or both, as feelings battled within her. But lashing out was easier than admitting to her feelings for him.

"You've been lying to me since Big Bear," she said, her voice quiet.

"I told you we were on the verge of a strike. The bigger question is why didn't *you* tell me you were on NegCom?" he asked, not altering his wide-legged stance.

"I did tell you, Ryan. It's not my fault that you passed out when I was talking to you last night and didn't hear me."

He ignored her admission. "They were using you. I can't believe you participated in something so unethical."

"Unethical?" she said, her voice rising. "I did no such thing. I'm a union member. I had the same right as anyone to be there tonight."

"Oh, you were the player to be named later?" he said. "They used the implicit threat of your family connections to browbeat the AMPTP into submission."

"I'm supposed to believe that the reputation of my little old daddy and uncle bullied a forty billion dollar industry into submission." She rolled her eyes dramatically, and propped her hands on her hips, chafing in her severe charcoal pants. "Please, Ryan, tell me something plausible."

"I just can't believe that *you* of all people would trade in on your family name. Did you want to be at the negotiating table that badly? Is this an ego thing?"

"I did not do anything wrong." She spoke slowly in case he'd lost half his brain cells. "The AMPTP hires all you folks from good schools and impressive law firms for one reason: to intimidate the hell out of whomever you're negotiating with. We did the exact same thing, that's all. Everyone on your side of the table knows that I wasn't going to whisper in Daddy's ear or Uncle Billy's about the strike. You know better than I that they would have to recuse themselves anyway," she said referring to a judge's obligation to take themselves off a case if they have any relationship to the participants. "I think the bigger issue here is why didn't you tell me what was going on? I asked you point blank and you gave me some BS about contracts and closing deals."

"Attorney-client privilege—"

She didn't let him finish. "I didn't fall off the turnip truck yesterday." She pointed a ring free finger at him. "I may not have gone to law school, but I wasn't raised on a dirt farm either. This is not the kind of thing covered by that. I know you couldn't tell me how much the AMPTP was willing to offer, but you could have mentioned that you were on the committee. I might have made a different decision."

She pulled the tight pearl encrusted barrette clip from her hair and dropped it on the dining room table. One by one, she undid her suit buttons and slid the jacket from her shoulders. She couldn't imagine how he did it, wear a suit every day. She'd done it for a few hours and the confinement almost killed her. She kicked off her black patent leather pumps and padded to the bedroom in sheer stocking feet. She carefully placed her suit on its special hanger and pushed it back into the far recesses of her closet, hoping she wouldn't have any occasion to wear it in the near or far future. Wearing only her pearls, her lacy white camisole, and tap pants, she walked, bare feet hitting the wood planks until she was back in the dining room. Ryan was still there, his arms dangling at his sides uselessly.

"I'm not going to argue with you anymore, Ryan. I'm tired as all hell and the dog and I are going to bed. I suggest you do the same—at your house." She stalked back to the bedroom.

"You can let yourself out," she threw over her shoulder before slamming her bedroom door to emphasize the point.

FOURTEEN

HER BEDROOM WAS another disaster in the making. Why was making clothing decisions so difficult these days? Sophie knew her life was at a crossroads. She looked at her choices for her father's party and cursed Selie for talking her into the co-hosting role. The appropriate dress hung under sheer plastic in the middle of the closet. She'd stopped at Nordstrom in the mall on the way home and picked it up. If this was growing up, she wanted none of it. The store's muted earth tones didn't match her multicolor personality. The dress was purely a Jackie O, Princess Grace number. The black gabardine sheath dress had a scoop neck with contrasting white piping. It hung with a matching car length coat with the same white edging. It was timeless, classy, and befitted the woman her parents raised her to be.

The dress she was itching to wear would set the country club set's tongues wagging. It was black and sheer, with a deeply scooped bodice, and a cut out that would showcase the full length of her spine. It left absolutely nothing to the imagination. With textured stockings, high, high heels, and jet black hair, she'd be the talk of party. She was the "rebellious one," after all. She had a part to play and she didn't want to let her family down.

She looked back and forth, back and forth, then at the clock. She needed to make a decision. A knock on the door startled her. She hoped it wasn't Selena here to check up on her. She would be as good as her word and show up —no matter how much the idea repelled her.

The dog squirmed with excitement, her nose pressed to the doorjamb. She looked through the peephole and her terrycloth shoulders dropped, resigned to the over-whelming emotion that always engulfed her when she saw him. Both excitement and dread warred within her. She pulled open the door. Ryan stepped in, his broad shoul-dered, narrow hipped body encased in an impeccably tailored charcoal suit and blue silk tie that mirrored his eyes.

He leaned down to kiss her hello and she turned her head, his lips brushing against her cheek instead.

"What are you doing here?" she asked, knowing she sounded unforgivably rude.

Ryan shut the door behind him, ignoring the dog jumping on his calves. "I'm here to take you to the party."

"I don't recall you being on the guest list."

"Your sister thought you may *forget* to invite me, so she called to make sure I'd be there."

Sophie cursed under her breath. Selena didn't trust her, so she'd done the next best thing—sent Ryan to make sure she toed the line. Sophie gestured to the couch, inviting him to sit. Looking down at her old terry robe, she said, "I'm not exactly ready. It's going to be a while. Maybe you should go home and come back when it's time to go."

Ryan didn't sit in the living room like a guest. Instead, he followed her to the bedroom. "I'm not going anywhere." His eyes were unreadable. A secondhand chair, its holes and tears obscured by large Indian cloths, enveloped Ryan's bulk.

"Ryan, how can you just waltz in here as if yesterday didn't happen?"

"What's done is done."

"And that's it. You question my motives, you question my judgment, and I'm supposed to be okay with that?"

"Maybe I was wrong," he said his voice practically a whisper.

"Excuse me, I don't think I heard you."

"I had a long and lonely night to think about this...us. I was wrong, and you were right, okay? You had as much right to be there as anyone else."

She stopped fiddling with the undergarments she'd picked up. "Why were you so mad?"

He sat up a little straighter in her chair, still looking ridiculously out of place. "Because unions fail people all the time, especially those who put their blind trust into the hands of crooked leaders. I think they're not protecting you like they should. If I were you, I'd be worried about the pension's poor performance, to start."

"Ryan, I'm not blind to the problems of unions, but on the issue of compensation and future earnings, I trust them. Trust *me* to know what I'm talking about.

"But I love you and don't want anyone to cheat you or use you."

Sophie's stomach flip-flopped. There was that word again. Ryan, her sister, her parents. It was almost too much. Determinedly, she played it as cool as a cucumber, and went back to getting ready.

"Which of those are you wearing?" He gestured to the open closet—the two dresses on prominent display.

"I can't decide," she answered honestly. "This one here," she pointed to the conservative dress, "is the right and appropriate and sane thing to wear." She pointed to the other. "This one will keep them talking for months."

"I thought this party was for your dad," he said quietly.

She looked at him quizzically. "Of course, it's in honor of another award or achievement or commendation he's won."

"Then why would you want to draw attention to yourself? That seems a little selfish."

Sophie did a double take.

"It's not like that," she stammered, though it was *exactly* like that. "Our family drama is like a little play and everyone must act their part. Dad will be the tyrant. Mom will be the peacemaker. Selena will be the perfect daughter, and I will be the rebel. That's just how it is. If I don't come dressed the part, the whole family will come unglued."

"You've changed, you know." He nodded sagely. "When I met you, you had more rings and studs than a gypsy," he said, his voice growing quieter, more thoughtful. "These days, your hair is natural more often than not.

Your clothes don't give everything away at first glance. Not every finger or hole has a ring."

She stepped further away from him, instantly wary. "Maybe you're trying to change me. Lawyers can be persuasive that way." Had she been manipulated? She'd thought he liked her, maybe even loved her, for who she was, but all along maybe he'd been trying to change her into his ideal girlfriend. She shook her head, clearing it a little. She and Ryan weren't together. Not really.

None of this mattered anyway.

"I think *you* want to change, Sophie."

When he spelled it out plainly and simply, she had to admit to herself that it was true. In the years she'd been on her own, she'd discovered who she was, and she liked herself. She no longer felt the need to put everything on display. It was enough that she acknowledged she was an artist and she was a little different from the average girl.

She pulled the department store bag toward her and pulled out nude stockings and a shoebox. About to untie her robe, she glanced up, realizing Ryan was still in the room.

"Do you mind? I need to get dressed if we're going to do this thing."

Ryan smirked. "O...kay. If that's what you'd like." Acting like a typical man, he dragged his butt leaving the room, clearly hoping to catch a glimpse of breast or a flash of thigh.

ONE HOUR and fifty-nine minutes later, Sophie emerged from the bedroom. Her hair was smoothed into a flapper-style bob with deep waves framing her small face. Her ears were unadorned except for small pearls at her lobes. Her makeup was subtle but perfect, and the dress fit her slim frame perfectly. The only bit of old Sophie that remained was her eyebrow ring. He didn't say a word about it, though. It was his Sophie and it wasn't her at the same time. He couldn't believe he'd always gone after hourglass brunettes with big boobs and wasp waists. Who knew this straight up and down redhead would grab his heart?

She screwed up her face and stuck her tongue out at him. "Stop staring," she said, her normally husky voice breaking with nerves. "It's still me under here. Let's just get going before I change my mind."

Ryan followed her careful directions to her parents' house in San Marino. He didn't know what he was expecting, but it was more—more landscaped, more gated —just *more* than he'd been ready to deal with. A private valet greeted them at the gate. Ryan handed over his keys. Behind the eight foot tall hedges and iron gates stood a stately Spanish house. Flickering lanterns flanked the wide flagstone steps leading to the house. Warm light poured from every window. The faint sounds of music and the tinkling of glasses drifted from inside.

He pulled the hand he had been using to guide Sophie from the small of her back and curled his fist into a ball of resentment. He didn't want to feel anger or jealousy, but the twin demons were there, released from the back of his subconscious where they lurked. How many times had he met his mother at one house or another just like this one —

doing his homework at a stranger's kitchen table while his mother scrubbed on her hands and knees?

It had incensed him as a child when the "woman of the house" would come downstairs and direct his mother to clean this or polish that, then disappearing to leisure time, the scent of expensive perfume lingering while his mom did the dirty work. On the car or, more often, bus ride home his mom smelled of cleanser and disinfectant, not Chanel No. 5, further amplifying the differences between the haves and have nots.

Sophie opened the unlocked door and looked at him.

"You coming?"

He schooled his features, hoping he hid his unease?

"You wanted to do this—so let's do this," she said, plastering a huge fake smile on her face and walking into the two story entrance.

He was surprised to find that the house had few guests. Soft classical music swirled around him from hidden speakers. Men and women in bow ties and black uniforms bustled about, carrying boxes of glasses and plastic-covered trays of food.

Sophie led the way past the mahogany staircase, its intricately curved wrought iron railing gleaming, to a kitchen. Selena stood perfectly poised in the midst of the chaos around her, directing the human traffic with practiced ease. Her graceful movements became animated when she spotted them. She hugged Sophie, but looked toward Ryan.

"Thanks so much for escorting my sister tonight. She looks lovely," she said, separating herself from Sophie carefully checking for anything that may have marred the spotless white dress.

Selena gestured at the ring in Sophie's brow.

Sophie shook her head, and Selena dropped the topic like a hot potato.

"Do you need any help?" Sophie asked, though it was clear that her sister had everything in hand.

Selie demurred. "Why don't you show Ryan around and get him a drink? The bartender is set up under the pergola in the back. Mom is bringing Dad in about half an hour. They plan to make an entrance."

"Of course," Sophie muttered under her breath. She grabbed Ryan's hand, though to him it felt like she was holding on for dear life. "Let me give you the five-cent tour."

So this was how the other half still lived. It was even newer and grander than the houses his mother had worked in. Everything, including housing, had been supersized. Ryan could have fit his mother's house into this place four or five times. Sophie showed him the formal living room where a wood fire roared. She made quick work of the finished basement and the family and dining rooms. Every surface gleamed. The furniture was impeccable. He felt like he was on the set of a nighttime drama. Real people didn't live this way.

"How many bedrooms are there?" he asked, more for something to say than for seeking knowledge.

Sophie counted on her hand quickly. "Five or six, depending on what you include," she said softly. She opened a door and showed him a sunny yellow room with a canopy bed draped with pale pastel fabric. "This was my room."

The room didn't reflect Sophie at all, at least the Sophie he thought he knew. "You lived in here?" He couldn't keep the incredulity from his voice.

She laughed. "It didn't look like this when I left for college, Ryan. I think in its last incarnation I'd painted the walls dark purple with some kind of ghoulish white mural on the far wall. Mom promptly had it redecorated after I left to something she found more...appropriate."

An older woman dressed sedately in yards of swirling purple crepe and low-heeled shoes burst into the room. "Sophie, my girl!" she cried excitedly. "Selie said you were here." She wrapped Sophie in a bear hug and kissed both powdered cheeks enthusiastically.

When the women parted, Ryan stuck out his hand tentatively. "Mrs. Reid, it's so nice to meet you." The room was quiet, and then the women burst out in laughter.

"Ryan this is our housekeeper, Faith Lawson. We just call her Lala."

Humiliation flooded Ryan. Of course this woman was her housekeeper. He should have known Mrs. Reid would not wear purple, or flat shoes. Of course the Reids were the type of family to have a housekeeper. Would he never learn?

Faith shook Ryan's hand. She looked him up and down appreciatively. "Well, well, you are a nice looking guy. Selie was right about that. Is it true that you're a lawyer?"

Ryan, inexplicably comfortable with this woman, nodded. "The rumors are true," he admitted.

· · ·

SOPHIE'S FACE burned with embarrassment. The chickens were certainly coming home to roost. How many times had she stood before her parents vowing to never be like them? But here she was, dressed like the perfect debutante with a clean cut attorney on her arm. It was just one night, she reminded herself. She was doing this for her sister and her parents. Despite their differences, she did love them. Doing this one little favor wouldn't change who she was. Just like seeing Ryan wasn't going to change her. Sophie vowed to remain true to herself and not buckle to Ryan's or her parents' influence.

Lala looked at Sophie. "This is very interesting. We'll have to talk about this later." She pulled off her shoes, her face awash in relief. "I just came up to change these shoes. I got downstairs and realized I looked like somebody's grandmother in these. I think I need something a little more jazzy for this occasion—you never know who may be out there," she said, giving Sophie a conspiratorial wink before padding from the room, the thick beige carpet muting her steps.

The noise from downstairs grew as the guests arrived. Sophie glanced in the vanity mirror and dabbed at her lipstick-stained cheeks with a tissue from the dresser. "It's show time. Let's get this over with."

They descended the stairs to find the foyer and living room filled with her parents' well-heeled friends. Sophie took a deep breath, released it, and then waded into the crowd. She hugged a lot of the women and shook hands with a number of the men, a big smile always plastered on her face. Gasps of surprise came from the celebrants as they remarked on how good she looked, how glad they were that she was out of that *nasty* rebellious stage, and asked her when she was going to quit her job and settle down with a nice man and have a few children.

A fork hit a crystal flute and the crowd was quiet. Wait staff wove through the throng, pressing champagne flutes into every hand. Then Sophie's parents entered. They were dressed elegantly — Sophie's mother Katherine wore a beautiful gray taffeta gown that underscored her elegantly upswept silver hair. Judge Reid wore a simple tuxedo with gray silk tie and cummerbund. Sophie and Selie drew up next to their parents. Selena shushed the crowd again.

"Thank you so much to everyone for making it here during this busy holiday season. My sister Sophia and I are so proud that the state bar association has seen fit to honor our father with a lifetime achievement award. He's given many excellent years of service to both the bar and the bench. Please join me in a toast honoring our father, Judge Harry Reid."

A chorus of "Hear, hear!" rose from the crowd. Glasses clinked and people sipped. Judge Reid stepped forward and the crowd quieted automatically.

"I just want to thank the three beautiful women in my life for helping celebrate this achievement. My lovely wife and life mate, Katherine," he said, placing a kiss on his wife's cheek. "And my lovely daughters, Sophia and Selena. Thank you."

He gathered Katherine and Selie around the waist. Sophie stood awkwardly next to her sister, and a photographer snapped photographs of the family. Muted applause broke out.

"Thank you, everyone. I won't give a speech tonight. Some of you who still practice hear far too much of me from the bench already." A few men in the crowd laughed heartily.

"Plus," he said, his blue eyes twinkling with merriment, "I think winning an award of this type means you have one foot in the grave, and I don't want to jinx my chances by being too satisfied. Thank you all for coming. Now go enjoy all of this food and champagne and good conversation."

In a rare moment alone, Sophie tipped back her second or third or fourth flute of the expensive champagne. She'd lost count while mingling with her parents' friends and their children—people she'd known from her neighborhood, the club, and various schools for years. She felt a warm hand on her back. She broke out in a smile, hoping Ryan had finally caught up with her. She turned only to have Alex Brewer at her back. She hoped her eyes didn't betray her disappointment, but Alex just smiled down at her, none the wiser.

He folded her into a friendly hug, and she kissed him on the cheek in perfunctory greeting.

"Alex, long time no see," she said amiably. She and Alex had graduated from prep years ago.

"I almost didn't recognize you. You look great."

"Thanks," she said. At a loss for something to say, she grasped at straws. She no longer had much in common with her prep school friends who had all become doctors, lawyers, or stay-at-home parents.

"Did you marry Sarah?" she asked after his longtime girlfriend.

"We broke up a year ago," Alex said. "I'd love to catch up with you, though. Maybe we could meet up for dinner next weekend?"

Flustered, Sophie was grateful when Ryan materialized at her side, his arm immediately snaking around her waist. She didn't know whether to kiss him or kick him for his obvious possessiveness.

"Ryan Becker." He thrust his hand toward Alex. "Nice to meet you. And how long have you known Sophie?"

Alex recovered gamely from Ryan's intrusion. "We go too far back to remember. She was my prom date, actually," Alex said, smiling at the memory. "She was dressed more like Elvira than a prom queen, but we had a good time." He looked at her in obvious appreciation. "This is quite a change."

"It was good seeing you, but as one of the hosts, I should circulate," she said and turned toward the large family room.

"AREN'T you going to introduce me to your parents?" Ryan prompted, having followed her out of the room.

Sophie turned back to face him, a pensive look on her carefully made up face. "Why don't we meet them now?" she said far too sweetly.

Her parents, champagne glasses in hand had just finished a schmooze session with another gray haired couple when they turned to Sophie.

"Mom, Dad," she started without preamble. "I'd like you to meet my…" She paused, clearly searching for the appropriate word. "My friend, Ryan Becker."

Ryan extended his hand into the firm grip of Judge Reid and then the soft grip of Mrs. Reid.

"I'm Judge Reid," Sophie's father said. "And this is my wife, Katherine."

Sophie's mother sized Ryan up. "So you're the one Selie told us about. It's nice to meet you."

Judge Reid's voice was gruff where his wife's was soft. "I hear you're an attorney. Where are you now?"

Ryan explained the particulars of his current position.

"VP, that's good. Where did you go to school?"

"I got my J.D. at Chicago."

"Mmmm, good school. Where did you summer?"

"Dad!" Sophie cried plaintively.

"It's my right to grill your boyfriends, Sophia. That damned actor was always too high or drunk to answer my questions."

Sophie's face reddened in embarrassment.

"It's okay," Ryan interjected, tightening his grip on her waist and tenderly kissing the top of her head. "I started at Bennett Friehauf downtown before going in house," he finished.

"Good man," Judge Reid said, heartily clapping Ryan on the shoulder. "Good man. Don't let this one scare you away. You'd be a very welcome addition to the family. Have you met my brother Billy Reid? It's never too early to meet the family and network. Should you ever want a change from corporate work, he can give you the inside track on federal labor law."

"Thank you, sir," Ryan said removing his hand from Sophie's waist and shaking Judge Reid's hand again. "I'll certainly keep that in mind."

Unfettered, Sophie stepped away from the small group. "Excuse me, I see someone I should speak with." She stalked, stiff backed, from the room.

"I'm sorry about that," Judge Reid said. He shook his head, resigned. "I've spent a lot of time apologizing for that girl. She's too damn sensitive about some things. What are your intentions toward my daughter?" Without Sophie there, Ryan squirmed under the scrutiny. Judge Reid continued without allowing Ryan a word in edge-wise. "Maybe you can set her on the straight and narrow path. You've been a good influence so far. When Selie told us about the co-hosting idea—we were half afraid Sophie would show up looking like a witch at Halloween. She doesn't look half bad, but I wish she'd take that damn thing out of her eyebrow."

"Harry!" Katherine exclaimed. "Be nice. Sophie isn't that bad. I'm sure she loves us. She just likes to do her own thing, I suppose."

"I love her no matter how she looks or dresses." Ryan's tone changed. "I would expect no less from her parents."

Katherine looked suitably chagrinned. "Of course. She's been a bit of a free spirit much of her life. But we'll be very happy if she settles down with someone like you."

Judge Reid interjected. "Marriage and children would be good for her. Then she could give up that crazy job— maybe she could go back and finish college when the kids are in school…"

Selena joined her parents then, diffusing the difficult moment. "Mom, Dad, did Ryan tell you how they met? It's a doozy of a story," she prompted. Judge Harry raised a curious eyebrow.

Ryan told the story of how they rescued Sasha on the freeway without embellishment. He didn't want to play up anything that would have her parents thinking he was some kind of crazy stalker. They were, after all, the parents of the woman he wanted to marry.

Katherine turned on her heel to look directly at her husband. "Don't you think now would be the time to tell Sophia the truth about Daisy?"

Selena looked from her mother to her father. "Is that the dog you guys got rid of after it peed on the Aubusson rug?"

The Reids didn't immediately acknowledge Selena's question. Ryan's mind flew back to the first time he'd kissed her after she'd cried in his car. Her gray eyes red from crying. She'd grieved for the dog for years and having Sasha had gone a long way to heal those old hurts.

"What truth?" he asked. "What do you need to tell her?"

Judge Reid crossed his arms across his middle, but remained silent.

Selena looked from her father to mother. "What in the heck is going on here?"

Katherine answered after a long silence. "We didn't get rid of the dog. Daisy had to be put to sleep because she was suffering from acute kidney failure. Somehow she'd gotten out into the garage and drank a half bottle of anti-freeze. When we called the vet, he told us we'd probably have to put her to sleep."

Selie gasped in surprise. "Why did you blame it on the dog?"

"Your father had come home to handle it. He knew how sensitive Sophie was and didn't want to upset her about the dog's death. So we made up that story." She looked at Ryan and Selie's stricken faces. "Don't be angry. She thought the dog went on to a better place, a better family—not the common grave of euthanized dogs."

Ryan was heartened by the fact that Sophie's parents weren't the evil people she'd made them out to be. But he knew they'd made a big mistake. "I know it's not my place to say anything. But your daughter thinks you dumped her dog without good reason."

Katherine looked at her husband, her blue eyes glassy with unshed tears. "I never realized... That was the start of her rebellious period, I think."

Judge Reid crossed his arms tighter and let out a loud harrumph. "That girl was going to be her own person no matter what, Katy. She was never going to fit into your mold like you wanted, like Selie. It would have been easier if you'd just accepted her as she was."

"Are you blaming this all on me? Who wanted to send her to private school starting in preschool? Who wanted her to go to Flintridge Prep, join the club, and play golf and tennis? None of that was me, Harry. Your children had to do all the *right* things. Maybe we haven't done the right thing by her." Katherine paused, looking first at Selena, then at Ryan. "I think we should talk to our daughter—starting with the dog. It's time she knew the truth." Harry looked at his wife, his eyes meeting hers for the first time. Katherine held out her hands and Harry loosened his grip on himself and put his hands in hers.

Their communication was silent, but Ryan knew they were coming to some kind of decision.

"Okay, I'll talk to her," Judge Reid said.

"No, Harry. We'll talk to her."

"I'll call her. I promise. Maybe she can come to the courthouse and I'll take her out to lunch like I used to in the old days."

Katherine's blue eyes steeled, and Ryan saw the strength Sophie's mother had to have to live with a personality as big as her husband's. "No, Harry. We're going to talk to her *now*. This whole thing between us and her has gone on far too long."

Harry glanced around helplessly. "We're in the middle of a party."

Selie spoke up. "Dad, these people have all known each other forever. They'll be fine for a few minutes. If anything comes up, Rob and I will handle it," she promised. When her parents didn't move, Selie looked from one to the other. "It's the right thing to do."

FIFTEEN

"YOU'VE BEEN QUIET." The drive home had been silent. It was like the luxury car came with a mute button. Sophie sat at the counter of her bungalow, perched on a barstool, still fully dressed.

"I don't have much to say, Ryan." She drew in a deep breath, releasing it on a sigh. "You've turned my life upside down in just a few months. First I broke my number one rule by dating an attorney, then I learn that my parents lied to me all those years ago."

"They wanted to protect you."

"Why are you defending them?" Her voice rose as her anger grew. "Would you lie to your children like that? Heap loads of guilt on them?" She bit off an unladylike curse. "White lies about Santa Claus or the Tooth Fairy I can understand. This…this was unforgivable."

"I agree that their actions weren't wise, but they had a good reason. They're your parents and they love you, Sophie."

His reasonable tone aggravated her. "Are you on their

side now? My dad must have loved you and your East Coast pedigree."

Though he winced, his reasonable tone continued. "What your dad thinks of me doesn't matter. It's what you think that's important."

She pointed to herself uncertainly. "Why me, Ryan?"

"Because I love you, Sophie Constance Reid—no matter how you look or what you do. I want to marry you someday. Mostly I want you to give us a chance—even if I *am* a 'suit.'"

"I don't know what you want to hear," she said, though she did know—like she knew her own name.

"This can't continue to be a one-sided relationship, Sophie."

"You're not being fair," she whispered. "It's not one-sided in bed."

"We're great together in bed." His voice grew rough with desire. "I love pleasuring you—having you pleasure me. Coming inside you is like the Fourth of July and Christmas all wrapped together. You turn me on like no other woman ever has. But that's not all of it. I can't go a few hours without thinking of you—how your day is going at work, how the dog is doing, whether your hair is blue or green or pink. I don't want to live without you."

"Live with me? Love me?" She blew out an exasperated breath. "You don't trust me."

"What are you talking about?"

Men really did have a one-track mind.

"The strike, Ryan. Or was it just another day at the office for you?"

"I'm willing to overlook your lapse in judgment when it comes to unions."

"Excuse me?" Her face heated up then. She was done with Mr. Reasonable. "I did not have a lapse in judgment —except for being with you. You're acting just like my father. You are not right just because you say so. Damn it, *this* is why I don't date lawyers. All that moral superiority BS. All unions are not corrupt, like all corporations are not perfect." Sophie turned her back on him. She would not let his good looks persuade her to do something she shouldn't do.

He laid his hands lightly on her shoulders, but she shrugged them off angrily. "There's nothing else to talk about, Ryan. It was great while it lasted, but we shouldn't see each other anymore."

"You're just going to throw away what we have?"

"We have great sex. That's all. There can be no relationship if you don't trust my judgment."

"Can I ask you something?" he asked, his tone anguished.

She shrugged.

"Do you love me? If this *is* all one-sided, please tell me now."

She wanted to lie—desperately. She wanted to close the door on hard decisions and real feelings. But the new Sophie—the person she'd recently discovered she wanted to be—wouldn't let that happen.

"It's not one-sided." It was all she could force past her lips.

His sigh of relief was audible.

"But why do we have to label this, Ryan? I like things the way they are."

"That won't work for me anymore." His tone brooked no argument.

"So where are we?" she asked, finally gathering the courage to turn and face him. The wisdom of age had taught her that love wasn't enough in a difficult world.

"Come to Thanksgiving at my mother's house."

"How does that fix this, us? Whatever we are…were to each other?"

"One more chance? We deserve that."

Sophie shook her head. "I can't do this. I already promised Holly I'd be at her house. She's going through a hard time right now. I need to be there."

"Give me—give *us*—the next two weeks. No talking, no pressure. I think we both need time to think. Let's plan to make some decisions on Thanksgiving. We'll talk after dinner."

She nodded.

"We'll do both, then. Okay?"

EVERY MOMENT they weren't working, Sophie and Ryan spent together. Every kiss said how right for each other they were. He coaxed her to keep her eyes open when she wanted to close them. Love shined in his eyes every time he entered her. It poured into her with every thrust. His persuasion was embedded in every glance, every caress, every orgasm they reached together.

Two and a half weeks later, Sophie dipped into the conservative side of her closet. She glanced in the bathroom mirror, hoping her clothes were appropriate for their Thanksgiving Day stops. She put on a simple A-line khaki skirt and a green cashmere twin set. They were going to Holly's place first, and her friends cared little about what she wore. She was dressing for Ryan's mother. She was about to slip some of her earrings out when she stopped. Scratch that. She refastened the highest loop around her lobe.

What in the heck was she doing? She hated that she was changing into the person she'd tried to escape for years. She was not going to change for anyone but herself. Determinedly she pulled off her country club clothes, kicking them to the side of the room with unnecessary violence. She was going to be herself. If anyone had a problem with that, then it was too damn bad. She'd done the right thing for her sister and her parents, but enough was enough. She wanted people to like her for who she was, end of discussion. She was done trying to be something she was not. From here on in, she'd dress how she felt and if that was natural hair, or blue hair, then so be it.

She reached in her closet and pulled out her black skin tight distressed jeans and a jet black form fitting sweater vest. She buckled a couple of skinny rhinestone belts around her middle, trying to create a waist on her tomboy figure. In deference to the cooler fall weather, she slipped on a cropped leather jacket that ended just below her breasts, and she was ready to go. In place of her usual sturdy work clogs, she slipped on three-inch platform shoes.

The quiet purr of the luxury car greeted Sophie as she left her house, locking the door behind her. She ignored

Ryan's appreciative wolf whistle and she slid into the dark interior of the automobile.

"I don't want to be late to Holly's," she said impatiently.

"Yes, ma'am," Ryan said, and drove the short distance to Holly's boyfriend's house in the hills.

Ryan ate a lot and Sophie ate very little. If she was worried about what her best friend would think about her showing up with Ryan, her worries were put to rest. Dominic's ill-timed announcement of Holly's pregnancy stole the show. Ryan holding her hand and cuddling up to her didn't even register on the radar.

A shot of nerves hit the pit of Sophie's belly as they turned from Reseda Boulevard onto Kittridge Street. She took a deep breath, not sure she should be apprehensive at all. She liked Ryan's mother Bridget, and it wasn't like she was out to impress her—that much. Looking down at her hands, she saw they were shaking with a fine tremor. The jitters were a manifestation of her fear that Ryan's mom and brother would read too much into the situation. It was something she'd have to get a handle on later that night. The stakes were too high—she didn't want to begin to think about what would happen *after* this meal.

"Have you been here before?" Ryan asked.

"I don't know anyone who lives in this part of the Valley."

Ryan pulled a face that held judgment.

"I'm done apologizing, Ryan. I am who I am. I'm not a bad person because I haven't spent every waking moment scouring the working class neighborhoods of Los Angeles."

She fumed. Silently, she regretted her characterization of his neighborhood. Maybe she was being a little judgmental herself. But she wasn't going to say she was sorry. He was making everything about this dinner and this relationship harder than it needed to be. The worry that somehow she'd upstage his family firmly planted in her mind.

He sighed. "I didn't mean it to come off that way. Were you going to say something before I — "

"Can you cool it with the handholding? Holly thought we were surgically attached back there. I don't want your mother to get the wrong impression of our relationship." He'd taken to holding her hand whenever they were out. He'd barely released her at Holly's house tonight. Not that she didn't enjoy the firm warm pressure of his hand or the low hum of arousal that came along with it, but she didn't want his mom to get the wrong idea. Parents had a way of getting their hopes up when young people acted too lovey dovey.

They made a left turn onto a little street called Wynne Avenue and pulled up in front of a modest sand colored stucco house. He turned off the engine and turned to her. "And what impression is that?"

"Ryan, I know how parents have a way of getting their hopes up, and I don't want your mom to confuse our..." she mumbled the next part, "...sexual relationship for something more substantial."

He was quiet while he unhooked his seat belt, and got out, easing his long legs from the car. He opened her car door and grabbed the hand she automatically extended. Damn manners did her in every time. They stopped in front of a low cedar fence and immaculate lawn. "I want something more substantial."

She saw the curtains twitch to the side, then fall back just as quickly. "Look, your mom knows we're here. Let's just go in and do this thing. We'll talk about the rest later." She pulled her hand from his once and for all, making sure her hostess gift occupied both hands.

The faded wooden door opened before they had a chance to knock. Ryan bent down and kissed the snowy white head of his mother. Sophie handed over the small bouquet she'd picked up earlier at the market.

"These are lovely flowers, Sophie. I'm so glad that you all could come. I know that you were busy with your other obligations, but I like to have my family around for the holidays."

They all bustled into the small living room.

Bridget's blue eyes twinkled as she got a vase for the flowers. "I think it's traditional for couples to alternate family holidays, so that everyone gets a little time with them." Sophie cast a knowing look at Ryan. He pulled his shoulders into a small "what-are-you-gonna-do" shrug.

Cameron, still in uniform, minus his Sam Browne belt, looked quite comfortable ensconced on the couch, watching a football game.

"Here," his mother said, motioning with her hand. "Let me take your jacket—though I can't imagine this little thing keeps you warm." She hung the small jacket on a too large hanger in the hall closet.

"Mrs. Becker—"

"I told you to call me Bridget."

She wasn't quite that comfortable with his mother

even after their cozy gabfest at brunch weeks ago. "Is there anything I can help you with? Dinner smells delicious." God, she sounded like a female Eddie Haskell. She needed to tone it down—a lot.

"No, no, dear. I have everything warming. Cameron will help me with the table. Ryan, why don't you show Sophie your room?"

Sophie felt like a teenager visiting her boyfriend's house for the first time. Walking into Ryan's childhood bedroom did nothing to assuage that feeling. As she wandered around the room, it was like peering into Ryan's past. The room had boy-blue walls and an old-fashioned, wooden twin bed. Posters of late nineties bands, whose hairstyles made her cringe with memories, covered the aging wallpaper. When she walked by the bed to peer at the photos on his nightstand, Ryan grabbed her hand and pulled her down on it with him.

On her back, looking into his earnest, handsome face looming above her, Sophie sighed inwardly. In her high school fantasies, she couldn't have imagined anything as sexy as this. Had she been able to see the future, she would have waited patiently for Ryan to come to her. She loved this man, plain and simple. She wanted to spend the rest of her life with him, have babies with him, grow old with him. The realization felt like a smack in the head. Thank God he spoke or she might have said something she would come to regret.

"I love your hair when it's natural like this," he said, fingering the golden red strands.

"Ryan, about the strike...shouldn't we—"

"Shh, let's not talk about that right now." He angled his corduroy leg between hers. "Just one kiss."

His lips met hers and it was like striking a match near tinder. She was aflame with arousal and need within seconds. From her prone position, she wrapped her arms around his neck, pulling him ever closer. His right hand unerringly zeroed in on her breast. He brushed his thumb across her nipple — already beaded with desire. Despite the layers of clothing between his hand and her body, a wave of desire had her closing her legs around his in a vice-like grip.

She heard a throat clear by the open door. "Dinner's ready, dears," she heard Bridget chirp. The door closed softly.

Sophie threw her arm across her face. "I can't believe you started this at your mom's house. I'm going to die of mortification out there."

Ryan eased back next to her on the narrow bed, waiting for his erection to subside. "I think she knows about the birds and the bees." He chuckled.

"That's not funny. I'm going out there before this gets any worse." Sophie pulled herself from the bed, opened the door, and stalked down the short hall back into the living area. Bridget had covered her dark wood table with a lacy tablecloth. Four places were set with what looked to be her best china and silverware.

"I know you probably ate a little something at your friend's house, but I couldn't resist making a few of the boys' favorites."

Sophie looked at the heavily laden table and hated to think what *all* of the boys' favorites would be. There was a turkey, of course, some kind of green bean casserole, and a few other sides. Then she looked at the buffet where more platters rested and she spotted two pies. Good thing she'd eaten lightly at Holly's.

"Are you sure there isn't anything I can do to help?" Sophie said, watching Bridget bustle about. Cameron hadn't budged from his spot on the couch.

"Why don't you come into the kitchen with me for a minute?" Bridget said, putting down a platter and beckoning Sophie. "I think there's something I could use help with."

Sophie followed her into the small kitchen, the swinging door closing behind them. "What can I—"

Bridget held up a hand. "Don't get me wrong, dear, I think you're a lovely girl." Bridget's tone did not bode well for the rest of this conversation. "And I think you make my son happy, but I need to know: are you serious about him?"

"Ah…" Sophie faltered. "We-we're just friends, ma'am," she began, stumbling over the words as she tried to be polite while masking her insecurity. "I-I'm not sure what you're asking."

"I think you understand me perfectly, hon." Bridget grabbed a fraying green and yellow flowered dishtowel from the oven handle and wiped some crumbs from the green tiled counter into the sink. "Let me say this, then. Ryan may not have said so, but he's a man who believes in marriage and family and lifelong commitment. He was engaged once before to a woman named Jocelyn. She was like you—pretty, rich, smart—but I think Ryan wasn't enough for her. He couldn't fit into her country club world of Bel Air."

A wave of emotions crashed into Sophie. She was sorry for Ryan if that woman had left him for such superficial reasons, but she was also jealous that she was obviously not the first woman he'd loved. Though it was irrational to think she would be at his age. She also wanted to howl in protest. They weren't giving her a chance. She wasn't like this Jocelyn. No matter what her upbringing had been like, she was down to earth and real. Her issues with Ryan—or relationships, for that matter— had nothing to do with him or his family or hers or Reseda or San Marino.

Mrs. Becker continued, "I just want what's best for my boys, and if you're not serious about settling down with him, please don't drag it out unnecessarily."

"I don't know what to say…" Sophie trailed off.

Bridget patted her bare arm. "There's nothing to say. I just wanted to get that off my chest." She placed a boat of gravy in Sophie's empty hands. "Let's get out there before the food gets cold."

Sophie made it through her second meal, taking decidedly tiny portions of food where she could. Ryan must have had a hollow leg the way he packed away his mother's cooking. Cameron ate heartily as well, contributing only monosyllabic answers to his mother's questions. Ryan's brother watched Sophie closely, though, making her uncomfortable with his scrutiny.

Ryan's family loved him and wanted to protect him. That was obvious. She wanted to declare that she wasn't the enemy. Nevertheless, the questions that plagued them nagged at her as well. What exactly was she doing here? With him? What had started out as a little sex play had gone too far. It would be best for everyone if she broke it off now before anyone got hurt. It was already too late for her. She could handle one broken heart, but not the guilt of two.

She was jarred from her reverie when Cameron and Ryan raised their voices over their dessert of sour cherry pie.

"Bro, I can't believe you're hashing over this ground again. What's done is done," Cameron said with finality. Turning away from Ryan, he addressed their mother. "Mom, do you need help with the roof?"

Bridget pulled herself up rigidly. "I think I can handle that just fine on my own," she said stiffly.

"Just because it's in the past doesn't make it any less fair, Cameron." To his mother, Ryan said, "Mom, if you would just let me look into it, maybe something can be done, legally."

"We've been over this a dozen times, Ryan. Sometimes things just don't go your way. I have the house. It's paid for. And I can always pick up some work if something happens."

Sophie watched Ryan practically grind his teeth in frustration. The thought of his mother scrubbing one more toilet or mopping one more floor must be twisting his gut. "The statute of limitations will come up soon, and I don't feel comfortable just letting them get away with what they did to you and all the other people relying on them."

She cringed inwardly. Conversations about money were for family only, and she was anything but family. "I can see this is a private conversation. Why don't I step outside for a bit..." She placed her paper napkin on the table and started to rise.

Bridget rose instead. "It's okay, dear. The topic is closed. Ryan just gets a little carried away sometimes."

"Mom, the topic is *not* closed." Ryan grabbed his mother's small, rough hand, holding it close to his heart. "You wouldn't be struggling and still pinching pennies if Dad's union hadn't stolen his pension money. You were counting on that, and you don't let Cameron and me give you much."

"I do just fine," she said proudly, disappearing into the small kitchen.

Sophie looked from brother to brother, their eyes locked in a battle of wills. She stood and gathered their empty plates and stacked them on the buffet. What in the hell was this about his father's union and a pension? In all her talk about the good things that unions do, he'd never mentioned this. It explained a lot about his questions about her total allegiance to the Local.

Bridget brought out cups and saucers. Sophie was glad that coffee passed quickly and uneventfully. She needed to go home and think about how she was going to quit her addiction to Ryan. They represented everything the other hated. He was never going to be something other than a lawyer, and she was never going to be anything less than a card carrying union member and totally free spirit. In spite of his pedigree, she loved him. He may be the right guy for her, but she was the wrong woman for him. Bridget thrust several Tupperware containers full of food at them. After they said good-bye, they finally made their exit and he pulled away from the curb.

"I'm sorry about the scene in there. I just want my mom to stand up for herself."

Pensions and unions were a sore topic between them, but Sophie couldn't help herself. "What happened to your mom's pension?"

Ryan sighed. "When my dad died, the shop steward, a good friend of my dad's, assured us that Mom would get death benefits and that she could count on Dad's pension when she came of age. She worked and waited, looking forward to a comfortable retirement, but when she applied for the annuity, we found out the union had gone bust."

"Isn't there some kind of government assistance for her, at least?"

"The government's Pension Benefit Guaranty only steps in if the union had paid the premium. Crooks don't pay for insurance."

"So…" Sophie paused, the import of his revelations sinking in. "Your mom has no retirement—at all?"

Ryan stopped short when a yellow light turned to red at Woodman Avenue. "Nothing, nada, zilch, zero. It'll be up to Cameron and me to supplement what little she'll get from Social Security."

"I'm sorry that your dad's union lost the money, but that doesn't mean all unions are bad and that all union leaders are crooks." It was the wrong thing to say at the wrong time, but she couldn't help herself.

All too quickly, Ryan turned up her driveway. He shut off the car and looked like he planned to come in. But before he could open his door, she put her hand on his arm, halting his movements. "I need to be alone right now."

"Sophie, we need to talk…about us."

"I couldn't agree more," she said, trying to appease him. "Just not now."

"Then when?"

She pushed open the door and stepped out, turning only to grab her small jacket from the seat. "I'll call you." She slammed the door. The only call she planned to make was one saying good-bye. She practically ran to her house, afraid if she turned around, she'd lose her resolve and invite her lover into her bed and her life forever.

SIXTEEN

RYAN PUSHED the car door as hard as he could, but the finely tuned foreign machine closed with a quiet snick. The garage door was the same. It lowered with quiet precision. Damn the handyman for fixing the kitchen door as well. It closed slowly, quietly, and securely. He looked at his pristine kitchen and spotless living room. There was nothing in this damn place he could take his frustration out on. Nothing punchable or kickable or even breakable.

Shame on him for making the same mistake twice. He was so sure that Sophie loved him, so sure that his background made no dents into her feelings for him. But reality was slapping him in the face right now. He'd taken her to his mother's house, told her the truth about his father, and he was alone again. He was crazy to have expected something different with Sophie. He just…had.

He dropped to the couch and threw his hands over his eyes. From the beginning, he'd known this whole thing with Sophie was temporary. She was cute and funny and sexy, but he'd never expected to fall in love with her. He got up and paced around the house, walking into each room, restless.

The ringing doorbell startled Ryan. His heart lifted, inflated with hope. Sophie had come to talk. First, he would make slow, sweet love to her—then they would smooth out the differences between them. Opening the door and finding a buzz cut, stockier copy of himself was a disappointment.

"What in the hell are you doing here?"

"Ah, the Becker family welcome," Cameron said, pushing past Ryan into the living room and flopping on the couch. He picked up the remote from the table and put another football game on the TV.

"Is your butt attracted to soft surfaces?" Ryan sat down at the other end of the black leather sectional. "I'm surprised to see you unglued from Mom's couch."

"I'm just taking a load off."

They sat in silence for a few minutes watching the game, though the sound was muted.

"Look, I'm for family closeness and all that," Ryan said, "but what in the hell are you doing here? I could have been in the middle of something."

Cameron made a show of eyeing the empty rooms. "Nah, I knew you'd be alone. Ma spooked that girl good."

Ryan stopped feeling sorry for himself for a minute. "What did she say?"

"Ma told Sophie that if she wasn't serious, she should leave you alone."

"Damn."

"She gave Yesenia the same talk. Sophie looked as shell-shocked as my ex. But Jessie was serious about getting married, so she was fine. I'm gathering that Sophie's not. She doesn't exactly seem like the marrying type."

Ryan buried his head in his hands. They were quiet for another moment.

"I think Ma feels bad. Before I left, she said to me that she thinks you're in love with her."

Ryan only nodded slightly.

Cameron turned up the game and they watched Alabama State pull out a last minute victory against Tuskegee with a successful onside kick. He muted the television a second time, only half watching busty models in the beer commercial.

"So?" Cameron asked.

"So what?" Ryan retorted, annoyed.

"What are you doing here and what is she doing—well, wherever she's doing it?"

The doorbell rang before Ryan could answer. *What in the hell?* Then he heard the neighbor's dog bark and an answering yelp from another dog. Sasha?

Sophie stood there sans makeup and jewelry in a tight little t-shirt and jeans. He wanted to pull a jacket from his hall closet and cover her. He vowed to buy her a bra.

She looked oddly unsure of herself. "Can I come in? Talk to you?"

He nodded and she brought the dog in. Spotting Cameron on the couch, she hesitated. "Oh, if you have company, I can..."

Cameron, more animated than he'd been all night, picked himself up from the couch.

"The game was over anyway. I'm outta here, bro." He

stalked to the door, acknowledging Sophie with a wink and a nod.

SOPHIE STOOD AWKWARDLY next to the small stone fireplace. When she and the dog had gotten in the car, she'd resolved to settle things between them once and for all—no matter how it ended. She couldn't live in limbo anymore.

While she hesitated, gathering her thoughts, Ryan spoke. "You came here to break up."

Unexpected tears flooded her eyes and she closed them when they threatened to brim over. She nodded.

Ryan came to her, gently grabbing her chin and tilting her head up. She took a shuddered breath when he wiped her tears away with his thumb.

"You know where I stand, Sophie."

"I don't know," she said quietly.

"I think you do know. What are you afraid of? Love shouldn't be this hard." His voice was rough.

Her stomach erupted in a flurry of nerves at the mention of love. She wanted to believe with all her heart that he loved her.

"I'm not going to change," she said.

"I'm not trying to change you."

"I don't want to get rid of my tattoo or my earrings or my jewelry or—"

Ryan put a single finger to her lips. "I'm not asking you to change a thing, Sophie. I love you no matter what color your hair is and no matter how much silver you wear. I'll love you no matter what."

"You say that now, but you're a lawyer and you need to entertain, go to events, wear normal clothes. I don't want to be that beauty pageant wife."

Ryan laughed. "You're beautiful to me, but I don't think anyone is going to mistake you for Miss Alabama."

She batted his hand away, annoyed. "It's not funny, Ryan. You met my mom. She's always beautifully dressed and well-mannered—she's been whatever my father needs."

"I'm not asking—"

"And he's been really successful. Whenever he invited other judges or politicians or whoever over, she did it all."

"Sophie. Stop. I'm not asking this of you. I fell in love with you the way you are. Just you. With blue or pink hair. With all ten earrings and the tattoo. I love all of it. Don't ever change for me. If you want to change—and *I* think you *do*—do it for yourself."

This was better than she could have hoped. Maybe she *could* keep Ryan and stay true to herself. "Are you sure?"

"Well," he said, smiling, "I do have one little quibble."

Instantly wary, her eyes widened. "What?"

"You could wear a bra."

"Um, I don't think you're paying attention. I don't exactly need…"

He brushed a thumb unerringly across a nipple. She shuddered with need. "I'm not blind, hon."

"Be serious," she said, though a small smile graced her mouth.

"Seriously, Sophie." He bent on one knee before her and took her hands in his. "I love you. I will always love you. Please trust me and trust yourself enough to give us a chance."

Sophie looked at his earnest expression and saw the love shining through his eyes. Her nod was almost imperceptible.

He seemed to hold his breath. "Is that a yes?"

She nodded, more emphatically this time. He stood and picked her up unceremoniously.

"Ryan! What are you doing?"

"Sealing the deal."

He carried her to his large bed, put her down. She tingled with anticipation as the weight of his body rested on hers. "I have to make sure you don't change your mind."

He placed his lips on hers, starting with a slow slide then building into more. The kiss went on for a long time. When they came up for air, she looked directly at him, her eyes meeting his.

"I won't." She smirked. "There's an innocent dog to protect."

ABOUT THE AUTHOR

JOLIE MOORE

Crazy Beautiful Love

I write crazy, beautiful love stories because I believe story-telling is magic. I love complicated heroines with secrets, strong heroes who fall hard, and a long winding road to happily ever after. When I'm not writing, I love to travel to witness the diverse tapestry of humanity, photograph the beauty of the world, visit museums, and watch live theater. I live in West Hollywood, California ten miles from the nearest airport.

♥

I'm the host of Fifty First Dates the Podcast. I haven't found my own happily ever after, but I'm not done look-ing. Join me as I try to find my Mr. Right or maybe Mr.

Right Now in Southern California. #50firstdates #joliemoore #crazybeautifullove